$18.00

X/14:

April Mae Manning
Series

UNACCOMPANIED MINOR

UNACCOMPANIED MINOR

HOLLIS GILLESPIE

F+W Media, Inc.

Published by
Merit Press
an imprint of F+W Media, Inc.
10151 Carver Road, Suite 200
Blue Ash, OH 45242. U.S.A.
www.meritpressbooks.com

ISBN 10: 1-4405-6773-5
ISBN 13: 978-1-4405-6773-5
eISBN 10: 1-4405-6774-3
eISBN 13: 978-1-4405-6774-2

Printed in the United States of America.

10 9 8 7 6 5 4 3 2 1

Library of Congress Cataloging-in-Publication Data

Gillespie, Hollis.
  Unaccompanied minor / Hollis Gillespie.
    pages cm
  Summary: On her fifteenth birthday, April Manning, whose family members all work for an
airline and who has been hiding by taking one flight after another, relates the events leading up
to her making a bomb threat on a jet.
  ISBN-13: 978-1-4405-6773-5 (hardcover)
  ISBN-10: 1-4405-6773-5 (hardcover)
  ISBN-13: 978-1-4405-6774-2
  ISBN-10: 1-4405-6774-3
  [1. Custody of children--Fiction. 2. Air travel--Fiction. 3. Runaways--Fiction. 4. Divorce-
Fiction. 5. Criminals--Fiction.] I. Title.
  PZ7.G4032Un 2013
  [Fic]--dc23
                                        2013032224

Cover image © 123RF.com.

This book is available at quantity discounts for bulk purchases.
For information, please call 1-800-289-0963.

PART I

THE INCIDENT REPORTS

WorldAir Accident and Incident Report
Flight 1021, ATL–LAX, April 1, 2013, 11:15 A.M.
FTA Telex number 880002215

Level 3 Threat
Flight attendant found note placed on seat 42A:
"There is a bomb on board this plane! Not kidding!"

Unknown Male
Tuscaloosa Homicide Incident Report
April 1, 2013, 11:54 A.M.

Incident # 880002145
Type of incident: Homicide.
Type of call: Disturbance—described as "debris" falling from the air. Upon arrival at the scene, "debris" was discovered to be a deceased male. The body landed on a blue Toyota Prius from what must have been an enormous height. The Prius is now demolished.
Address of incident: Whole Foods parking lot, 1099 Roosevelt Ave., Tuscaloosa, AL.
Subject class: Victim, unknown male, Caucasian, approx. 5'10", 180 lbs.
Identifying marks: Three black crows tattooed on neck. Writing on back of shirt in red marker: "WorldAir flight 1021. We are being hijacked. Please don't shoot us down! Call 404-828-8805."

WorldAir Accident and Incident Report
Flight 1021, ATL–LAX, April 1, 2013, 12:01 P.M.
FTA Telex number 880002216

Level 4 Threat
Flight Deck has been breached.
Tower lost cockpit communication with WorldAir
L-1011 flight 1021 at 11:50 A.M. Homeland Security notified
11:52 A.M. Countermeasures deployed 11:59 A.M.

FBI Telephone Conversation Transcript
404-828-8805
04/01/2013, 12:20 P.M.

[phone ringing]
Unknown female:
Hello?
Agent Anthony Kowalski:
Who the hell is this, and why is this number written on the
chest of a dead FBI informant?
Unknown female:
He was an FBI informant?
Kowalski:
I'll ask the questions, kiddo! Who the hell are you?
Unknown female:
My name is April Manning. I'm on WorldAir flight 1021. You
lost all cockpit communication with us about twenty minutes ago.
Kowalski:
How the hell do you know that?
April Manning:
Because I'm the one who destroyed the airplane's radio signal.

PART II

THE ACCIDENT REPORT

Preliminary Accident Report
WorldAir flight 1021, April 1, 2013
Present at transcript:
April May Manning, unaccompanied minor
Detective Jolette Henry, Albuquerque Police Department
Investigator Peter DeAngelo, NTSB

My name is April *Mae* Manning—M-a-e, not "May" as in the month. The investigators had it wrong, incorrect, on the police report, and the distinction is probably important. I pointed it out to them because I just wanted to make sure they knew I was cooperating here, okay? And, by the way, I stated from the start that I know bombs are a bad idea. A very, very bad idea.

Investigator DeAngelo:

Okay, let's try to focus on the events as they transpired, shall we?

April Manning:

Bomb *threats*, though, have their uses—they really do—and I could probably expound on that later. First, I want to point out that if everything had gone according to the WorldAir flight attendant manual, we would not have been looking at such a disaster here. And I say "disaster" only to quote the president of the airline, because I overheard him outside the interview chamber just now shouting about what a "disaster" all of this is. Why don't they just call this an "interrogation" chamber? That's what it is, isn't it? I seriously hate euphemisms.

DeAngelo:

The question was, how did you break into the cockpit?

April Manning:

Let me explain from the beginning. So, here's the deal. We see things differently, the WorldAir president and I, about this so-called disaster. It could have been much worse, if you ask me, and that is really what you should be asking me, as opposed to *interrogating* me. By the way, right now I'm practicing the recommended co-parenting method of disagreement. That's to say, "We see things differently," as opposed to screaming and engaging in acts of petty-to-midlevel violence, like the time my mother drove Ash's new Jeep through the sunroom, or when Ash backed a dump truck over my mom's freshly planted azalea bushes to fill her swimming pool with pea gravel. I don't think the instructions of the co-parenting counselor stuck very well with either of them, but I personally like this particular piece of advice, to say, "We see things differently." I use it all the time, because for one it really does dissipate arguments, and for another, the mere utterance of the phrase infuriates each of my parents.

"Your future stepmother is getting promoted to partner in her law firm," Ash would e-mail me. "She says it's important for you to be at the banquet."

"We see things differently," I'd respond, prompting a barrage of vitriolic e-mails in return.

Just to be clear, I'd been told by the family court-appointed specialist that the hateful thoughts I have for Ash and his girlfriend are normal, which was a relief, because I'd spent way too much time on them. Especially after I read the guardian ad litem's report that was submitted to the judge. A guardian ad litem, or GAL, is someone appointed by the judge during a divorce case to write a report recommending who gets custody of the kids, and it's all based on what is supposed to be in the best interests of the child. In my case, the GAL said she had interviewed me, which was funny because I never met her, ever, and I'm not exactly a forgetful type of person. To say the least.

For example, I still remember my real father, and I was barely five when he died. He was a WorldAir flight attendant as well, and I remember the morning he left to work a flight to Orlando. I know it was Orlando because we'd just gotten back from Disney World and I begged to go back with him so badly that I almost got my way. He had already caved and was at his computer to check the counts on the flight to see if Mom and I had a chance of getting on.

But the flight was oversold. "Dang. There's two high-school groups and a giant mess of cruise passengers. Maybe next time, Beanie Baby," he said to me. He had a lot of nicknames for me. I remember them all: Beanie Baby, Bean, Taz (short for Tasmanian Devil), Dimples (I have some), and so on. (I was *five*, okay?) The morning he left he kissed me on each of my eyelids and told me to take care of my mother. I promised I would. That was ten years ago. And I kept the promise, too, believe me. I'm still trying to keep it, because it's a big responsibility that comes with being the last of a pedigreed airline lineage.

That morning, my father also gave me a foreign coin that was silver but for a small gold circle at the center. He said it reminded him of his two girls, Silvy and Goldie. Goldie is another nickname for me because of the color of my hair, and he called my mom Silvy sometimes on account of the color of hers, and you have to admit it is kind of unusual for the two of us to be silver- and gold-headed. My mother used to have hair my color until she had me, then it started growing out all shiny and silver. Not gray, but silver. Platinum. Looking like it was dyed that way. She wanted to dye it back to blonde but my father begged her not to, and I don't blame him; it was the prettiest color hair I'd ever seen. People constantly complimented her on it, and when she put on her uniform she always wore her hair in a thick French twist fastened in the back with a small chopstick. I guess when your hair is really thick you don't need much to keep it nice and knotted. Me, I wouldn't know. Mine's like corn silk, a bunch of hair but thin. She had a lot of pretty hair sticks. Dad picked them up for her whenever he worked a flight to Japan.

And another thing: my mother did not use the regular-size chopstick, but the kind made for little Asian children's hands. The other kind were too big; they stuck out too far. I'm not getting off-track here. All this is pertinent information. It's "germane" to the topic. I had to look up the word "germane" when I read the guardian ad litem's recommendation. It stuck in my head.

When she married Ash, he pressured her to dye her hair.

That's why it matches mine again. That's why I can use her badge.

DeAngelo:

April, the cockpit? How did you get in?

April Manning:

I can't take all the credit. I had help from my friend Malcolm Colgate. It's ironic, because Malcolm always used to tease me for being super-hyper safety conscious. For example, I hate it when passengers grumble about having to put their seats and tray tables upright during takeoff and landing. The extra three inches of velocity of a reclined seat during an impact could mean the difference between snapped and unsnapped neck vertebrae. And that lowered tray table? It could cause a spontaneous appendectomy. I don't want to be slipping and sliding all over the paralyzed and bisected body parts of these idiots while I'm trying to outrun the ball of fire coming through the fuselage.

"I can't believe you're afraid to fly," Malcolm liked to tease me. "Oooh, what's that? I think I smell smoke!"

"I'm not afraid to fly!" I'd protest. It's true. I'm not. It's just that you can't come from a long pedigreed airline lineage without hearing all the stories. Like how that big crash in New Orleans in the late seventies could have been avoided if only the ground crew had put the correct fuel in the tanks. Or how that giant crash in Mexico City happened because the idiot air traffic controller directed the pilot to land on a runway that was under construction. Like I said, I have a hard time trusting people, and almost all airplane crashes are due to stupid things people do. Just thinking about it would make me ask Malcolm if I could hold

Captain Beefheart, the emotional support dog he always got to bring onboard with him. Lately Malcolm has gotten into the habit of just handing Beefheart over to me as soon as we got situated in our seats. I am grateful for that. That dog is oddly calm. And I think he purrs. Can dogs purr?

Inspector DeAngelo:

I don't think so.

April Manning:

I swear this one does. Anyway, Malcolm and I like to compete with each other on our knowledge of airplane wrecks. I consider it extreme flirting. Maybe I should let him win once in a while, because he seriously couldn't hold a match to me.

"Dallas, flight 191," he challenged a few months ago as I took my assigned seat next to him.

"What is this, amateur hour?" I smiled. "Wind shear. Lockheed-1011 TriStar. The second biggest death toll involving an L-1011 in history." The legacy from that crash has probably saved thousands of lives since then.

Inspector DeAngelo:

What's the legacy?

April Manning:

The legacy is that now all aircraft are equipped with Doppler radar that can detect changes in wind patterns as well as weather patterns.

"Right?" I asked Malcolm.

"Correct," he applauded me.

Malcolm and I had started including the legacies of plane wrecks after a deadheading pilot once joined our conversation and informed us that, on certain DC-9s, you could still find raised Braille-like symbols on the strips right below the overhead bins that were meant to allow passengers to feel their way out of a smoke-filled cabin, should the need arise. Well, naturally the day came when a DC-9 crashed and the need arose. Then the National

Transportation and Safety Bureau (NTSB) discovered that, because smoke rises, the last thing they wanted was passengers standing up filling their lungs with it as they groped for tangible indicators to guide them to safety. After that the indicators were put along the floor, such as the "white lights that lead to red lights indicating the exits" strips you hear about in the safety demonstrations of some older-model jets.

But then of course an air crash came that tested the newer method, and it was discovered that, while smoke rises, noxious fumes *sink*. So the least desirable place now for passengers in a crash situation was for them to be groveling with their noses to the ground, inhaling the poisonous fumes billowing down from the melting synthetic polymers airlines use to manufacture their seat covers. So today the standard is for planes to have indicators that light up at "armrest level," because that air—between the rising smoke and the sinking fumes—*that* air is the safest. Or at least it is until we learn differently.

So it was the "legacy" of each plane wreck that allowed for that much safer air travel afterward, and so on and so on, because in the end air travel is really just a giant ongoing human experiment. I suspect Malcolm finds it fascinating because he is a boy and that's how his mind works. I am fascinated by aviation disaster legacies, of course, because my real father died in a plane crash.

Or I should be specific and say he died "due to" a plane crash, because, of course, he survived the impact; almost everybody on board did. But instead of jumping down the inflatable slide to the safety of the tarmac below, my father went to assist some passengers in the back of the plane whose evacuation was being obstructed somehow—and that was it. The fuel in the wings ignited and the plane was engulfed before the firemen could unroll their hoses. Anyone who hadn't made it out by then didn't make it at all.

And the obstruction that impeded the evacuation? A few passengers were clamoring to get their bags from the overhead bins. I guess some people have no "situational awareness," as the flight attendant handbook instructs us about. They think they have time. They don't understand the obvious dangers. My father understood the dangers, though, and still he went back to urge them forward. One wrong step is all it took. In instead of out. Forward instead of back.

Today, when flight attendants attend their mandatory annual training to update their skills, among the set of crash commands they are instructed to shout during impact—commands such as "Heads down!" and "Get up! Get out!"—there is a new command, and that command is "Leave everything!"

In the number of airline accidents since, it comforts me to think my father contributed to the revised safety measures that may have saved some people. This is another reason I am so obsessed with safety. My father literally died for this, so every time I badger a fellow passenger to put up their tray table or secure their carry-on or whatever, I am honoring my dad's legacy.

I was glad to see Malcolm on my flight, because I could never be sure he'd be booked. Unlike the gate agents, I can't pull up the passenger names. I can only pull up the crew manifests to see who is working the flight, which is why I can almost always book myself on a flight that Flo is working. But in Malcolm's case, I know how to decipher patterns, and Malcolm's parents have a pattern of putting him on late-afternoon flights on large-body aircraft. I suspect it's because they are using their frequent-flyer miles, and the bigger the airplane the bigger the likelihood for frequent-flyer seats.

Unaccompanied minors are usually seated together or with an employee flying nonrevenue if possible, so Malcolm and I are often assigned seats next to each other. Along with plane-wreck trivia, we like to compare divorce notes. For example, during his supposed interview with his court-appointed guardian ad litem, she gave him some Sharpie markers and said, "I hear you like to draw," and that was it, the whole interview. Then his dad's private investigator produced pictures of the GAL engaged in acrobatic sex with Malcolm's mother's attorney in the front seat of his Lexus. The judge of course threw out the report and his dad got shared custody. It's why Malcolm is always on the plane like I am. Our parents live across the country from each other. It's why we're always flying back and forth. It's also why we both go to the same school, an online academy that is part of the Atlanta public school system. It's the only way we can stay current in our studies while bouncing from coast to coast.

The difference between Malcolm and me, of course, and I'm sure you knew this, is that Malcolm flies full fare, while I fly nonrevenue. Still, though, he is the only friend I have who relates to my parenting situation.

PART III

THE GUARDIAN AD LITEM

FBI File Documents
1. Personal letter and court document, augmented
Received by Fulton County Judge Jonathan Cheevers via UPS, postmarked 12/13/2012
Custody recommendation of Catherine Galleon, guardian ad litem re Manning vs. Manning Fulton County Family Court Case # 708621
Red-marker margin notations inserted post submission by April Mae Manning

Dear Judge Cheevers,

I discovered the following document in my mother's e-mail account. (I admit accessing her e-mail may be considered delinquent, but since she has been committed to a mental institution and declared unable to care for herself, I acted in her interest as her next of kin.) The document is the report submitted to you by Catherine Galleon (my supposed guardian ad litem) regarding my custody. If you recall, you ruled in favor of her recommendation and granted my stepfather full legal custody and shared physical custody. I am resubmitting her report to you with my own notes in the margins.

Anyway, I think it's important that you understand a few things, so I made a list (my friend Alby Madison helped me with this letter. She's almost a lawyer). (She advised against the strong language, but we saw that differently):

1. I never met or spoke to Ms. Galleon. I think this is important, considering she invented a conversation we had.
2. I'm almost 15 years old, not 12. I think this is important considering Ms. Galleon is charged with minding my welfare. (Don't you think she should know how old I am?)
3. My stepfather, Ash Manning, is a lying, greedy, odious sociopath.
4. I don't play the guitar. I have *never* played the guitar.

Sincerely,
April Mae Manning
cc: Elizabeth Coleman Manning
—

Enclosure:
Guardian ad Litem Catherine Galleon
Report on Recommendation of Custody, Manning vs. Manning

April Mae Manning (hereafter referred to as "Child") is a vivacious 12-year-old girl [*I'm 15 almost!*] who is the subject of the Fulton County custody case Manning vs. Manning. She is in the seventh grade [*Eleventh grade level!!*], has an extremely high IQ, and is regarded favorably by her schoolteachers. [*What teachers? My high school is a computer.*] Her favorite pastime is playing the guitar. [*I don't play the guitar!*] I interviewed Child the morning of January 4, 2013 [*I never met this crazy shebeast!*], at Father's residence and she expressed great affection for Father [*He is not my father!*], while appearing fearful of Mother [*Not true!*]. It is my recommendation as Child's GAL that she not testify in chambers to Judge Cheevers because of her fear of Mother. [*I am not afraid of my mother!*]

Elizabeth Manning (heretofore and hereafter referred to as "Mother") is a flight attendant for WorldAir. She constantly refers to Child as "my daughter," as opposed to "our daughter," which would be more appropriate. [*Again, Ash Manning is not my father!*] For example, during mediation and interviews, she often declared "I love my daughter" and "my daughter needs me," causing me to remind her that this was about the Child, not about her. [*Since when is it selfish to say you love your kid? And I do need her!*]

Mother was extremely oppositional to my preliminary recommendation put forth during mediation, which would have given Mother a generous visitation schedule of Thurs. to Sun. twice a month [*Generous? Really? We see that differently!*], which Mother refused to cosign despite several warnings from me that I would recommend something a lot less lenient should this go to trial.

I found it detrimental to Child's interests that Mother would not agree to my recommended custody schedule even though I made it clear that I felt this schedule was best for Child. *[What do you know about what's best for a kid? I bet you can't even keep a goldfish.]* Mother's insistence for more time with Child is evidence she is putting her own needs above that of Child. Mother is self-focused in conversation, as is evidenced with the innumerable outbursts of "I love my daughter" and "my daughter needs me."

Mother's employment as a flight attendant ensures she is often out of town, a situation that is less than ideal for Child. *["Mother" only worked trips outside of her custodial time.]* Mother's employment reflects numerous disciplinary incidents.

When asked to describe Child's hobbies and attributes, Mother named a long list, but nowhere on it was Child's passion for playing guitar. *[I don't play the guitar!]* It appeared Mother did not know Child even played the guitar. *[I don't play the guitar!!]* When asked to cite names of Child's classmates, Mother was unable to. *[Maybe that's because I have none.]*

Mother took Child to get her ears pierced, which is a major medical procedure that she failed to discuss with Father beforehand. *[Seriously?]* I consider this a change in circumstance, and constitutes a viable reason to reconsider custody.

Ash Manning (heretofore and hereafter referred to as "Father") *[He is not my father.]* is a pilot for WorldAir. He loves his daughter very much *[I am not his daughter.]*, and constantly says so. *[But when "Mother" says it she's "self-focused"?]*

Father married Mother in 2004, soon after her first husband died in the WorldAir plane crash in the Florida Everglades, and subsequently legally adopted Child. I think it was immensely generous of him to marry a widow with a dependent child. *[Did I blink and wake up in a book by Charles Dickens?]* He is extremely loving and gentle when it comes to Child. [*He makes me sleep on the floor in the laundry room!*] Father's employment as a pilot often requires him to leave town, but he devotes much attention to assuring Child is accommodated during these absences. [*I could be getting dismembered by Satanists for all he cares!*]

Father has taken Child to a plastic surgeon to estimate correction of a large, disfiguring scar on Child's right arm. I find that very loving and considerate of him. [*That scar is his fault, he was just trying to cover it up so it wouldn't match the police report! And by the way, ear piercing is a "major medical procedure," but plastic surgery (!!) is not??*]

Father has interfered with Mother's employment in the past, most notably by, on a few occasions [*It was every day for a month.*], physically restraining her from leaving the house [*She missed work—the reason for the "numerous disciplinary incidents."*]. But he has apologized for that [*Really? To whom? Not to me or Mom!*] and promises never to do it again. [*Like crap!*] In any case, Father assured me his actions were instigated by his concern for Mother [*Like crap!*], who was exhibiting signs of mental instability. [*Like crap!*] Afterward, Mother filed charges against Father and had the court issue a temporary restraining order against him, causing him to be evicted from the family residence. I found Mother's actions to be harsh and overreactive. [*Is she headless?*]

When asked to name Child's likes and hobbies, Father extolled Child's love of playing the guitar he bought her [*What guitar? I don't play the guitar!!!*], and how teaching her melodies on it comprises important father-daughter bonding time. [*Ash Manning has taught me NOTHING! Except maybe distrust.*] I find this very touching. [*Seriously, is this GAL headless?*]

Based on my research, I recommend FATHER retain full legal and physical custody of CHILD, and MOTHER's time be limited to four hours supervised visitation every other Thursday from 4–8 P.M.

Respectfully submitted,
Catherine Galleon, Esq.
[Judge Cheevers, here is a list of reasons why this recommendation should be thrown out and your decision reversed immediately:

1. *Like I said, Ash Manning is a lying, greedy, odious sociopath.*
2. *Catherine Galleon is an ignorant succubus.*
3. *My mom may not be perfect, but she cares about me and I am at least RELATED to her.*
4. *If you don't fix this soon I will bomb a plane. I am not kidding. I never threatened to bomb anything when my mother had full custody, did I? This is a new development in my behavior! This constitutes a CHANGE IN CIRCUMSTANCE!]*

PART IV

THE STATEMENT

WorldAir Aircraft Accident Report
Lockheed L-1011, flight 1021, ATL–LAX, April 1, 2013
Passenger Summary

Name: April Mae Manning
Birthdate: 4/1/1998
Status: Unaccompanied Minor, Nonrevenue
Seat number: 42B, Mid Left Jumpseat, Lower Galley
Jumpseat, Cockpit

Statement:

One of my most prized possessions is an official WorldAir flight attendant manual, even though I can't really consider it my possession since I stole it from my mother. But even she can't officially consider it her possession, since it's government issue and, because it contains high-level in-flight security information, she is expected to return it when she quits or retires (or gets fired, but Flo said that's not going to happen). Anyway, I cherish this manual because I come from a long pedigreed airline lineage from both my mother's and father's sides of the family. (And I mean my real father, not Ash Manning, who is not my real father no matter what he tells you.)

My grandfather Roy on my father's side had been a World-Air employee so long that he and the CEO of the company—the same Mr. Alan Bertram outside the door right now hollering about what a big disaster this all is—he and my granddaddy Roy go way back, literally to day one. They had both been hired as engineers on the same date, and remained close friends up until the day my grandfather died. But where Mr. Bertram was a corporate type, my grandfather was a laborer. He loved to work with his hands. Friendships are thick, though, and Mr. Bertram himself attended my granddaddy's funeral and stood in the receiving line like everyone else. He gave my mother his card, telling her to call him if she needed anything.

My grandfather on my mother's side, Maxwell Davenport, was a baggage handler for Spartan Airlines back before it merged with WorldAir, and he met my Grammy Mae (see? M-a-e) right on the tarmac of the Monroe County Airport as she was greeting passengers about to climb the jet steps to a flight to Atlanta. My grandmother is sixty-two now and still a flight attendant for ExpressAir, a regional affiliate for WorldAir, a factor that is due to no small feat. Grammy Mae had been canned back in the seventies for having the audacity to get knocked up with my mother's older brother, so she sued the airline for discrimination and won a precedent-setting case that enabled the mandatory rehiring of all stewardesses previously fired for being pregnant, or over the age of thirty or—I swear this is true—*getting married.* Any one of those three factors used to be a perfectly acceptable terminable offense until Grammy Mae and a collective of other strong-minded and unfairly fired stewardesses descended on the Supreme Court and set it right.

Today Grammy Mae still flies domestic routes and stays busy. Her favorite trip is the thirty-four-hour Las Vegas layover on the 757, because the crew is put up at the Silver Spur Hotel and Casino where they get a coupon book that includes two free welcome cocktails and half off at the Rootin' Tootin' breakfast buffet.

"It's like a mini vacation," she tells me. "I can't believe I get paid."

She welcomes the breaks, because she told me when she's not working, my Papa Maxwell expects her to be a farmer's wife. He retired early from his baggage-handling job and now runs a vegetable stand along Riverside Road, south of the Atlanta airport. Maybe you have heard of his stand; it's called Papa Maxwell's Fresh Fruit & Produce. He's kind of famous for his homemade ginger ale, brewed using the ginger root he grows in his garden.

He keeps bottles of it on ice right by the cash register, and people come from miles around to buy it.

I used to like to sit under pomegranate trees in Papa Maxwell's backyard and feast on the fruit, with the ruby-colored juice running down my arms and dripping off my elbows. This is where they found me, by the way, on that Easter Sunday when it was time to tell me what had happened to my real father. I was under the pomegranate trees, gathering the fallen fruit into my lap.

My mother had been a flight attendant since two years before I was born, then flew with me in her belly until she was so pregnant it was against policy for her to continue. But being in the air was the only thing that made the morning sickness go away, she said.

"I don't know what it was, but once the plane took off all of a sudden I could feel you quiet down in there," she would tell me. "It was like reverse gravity or something. Suddenly I felt light as a feather, like the weight of the world was lifted. I loved flying when I was knocked up." Then she would kiss me goodnight.

She called them "sky stories," and she told me one every night before bed, even after she married Ash, who thought she was ruining me with this ritual for some reason. "She needs to toughen up!" he'd shout at her, often while standing over us as she held me in bed. "You're ruining her!"

They always fought, until he figured out how to shut her down. He liked to throw open the door to my bedroom, grab me out of bed, and shake me at her. "Let's play shaken baby syndrome!" he'd shout. I wasn't exactly a baby, but I'd be wailing like one, and she would instantly back down and beg him to hand me to her. But he wouldn't. He would just shove me at her, and then yank me away. "Shaken baby syndrome!" he'd laugh. He was such a bastard.

Inspector DeAngelo:

Don't cuss.

April Manning:

28

"Bastard" is technically not profanity. Bastard. Bastard. Bastard-ass bastard! She tried to lock my bedroom door to keep him away from us, but he kicked the door down. That explains the scar on my arm. The door hit me, threw me against a bookshelf, and broke my commemorative Wonder Woman plate. I woke up in the hospital with a concussion and six stitches in my arm.

Inspector DeAngelo:

Didn't your mom call the police and have him arrested?

April Manning:

That's a good one. The police were called, yes. I recently read the report, which was attached to the recommendation on custody. My mother made the mistake of telling Ash to call 911 while she tended to my injuries. Ash called, all right, but he told them my mother was the one who hurt me. When the police came, it was her word against his. I was unconscious from getting bashed in the head by a door, which made it pretty hard to put in my two cents. The officer took their statements in the emergency room while I was getting stitched up, and since both were claiming abuse against the other, the officer had them both hauled off to jail.

Wanna know what happens to an unaccompanied minor when she's released from a hospital emergency room while her mother and stepfather are in prison and all her grandparents are on a cruise ship in the middle of the Atlantic? She gets thrown into the Fulton County Children's Shelter, which is just a euphemism for juvenile jail, because that's where they also throw the runaways, junior druggies, muggers, thieves, and any other criminal under the age of eighteen, male *and* female. It took three days for things to get sorted enough so that I could go home, and I had to spend most of that time barricaded in a utility closet to keep from getting assaulted by a two-hundred-pound seventeen-year-old thug who had decided I was his "bee-otch."

After that, Ash called 911 on my mother all the time. It was his favorite thing to do. The police would be at our door in minutes, Ash would make up some complaint and demand they write a report. When my bedroom door was replaced, he put the lock on the outside of the door. That's how he started locking us up. I used to have to climb out the window and onto the porch roof to get out of the house. Then I couldn't get back inside, so suddenly I was a runaway and it was all my mom's fault, according to that crazy bitch the guardian ad litem.

Investigator DeAngelo:

Cussing.

April Manning:

"Bitch" is not profanity. They say it on television all the time. Even daytime TV.

Anyway, Ash thought it would do me good to let me lie alone, crying in the dark. Also, it wasn't until she married him that we began celebrating Easter Sundays again. Until then we ignored Easter. The purpose was to try to keep me from remembering things. It was a diversionary tactic employed by my mother. Ash thought it was ridiculous and was certain it wouldn't work. He was half right; it didn't work. I still remembered that my real father died on Easter. But I didn't think it was ridiculous. Like I said, diversionary tactics have their purpose.

Speaking of diversionary tactics, I really think they should include ways to recognize the difference between smoke bombs and actual bombs in the "Explosive Device Recognition" guide in the WorldAir flight attendant manual, which is like my bible. But like with the real Bible, I still have my criticisms of it. I will probably expound on those later, but for now, according to the "Explosive Device Recognition" section, the list of things to look for in a suspicious device is:

1. Power source
2. Initiator

3. Explosive (of course)
4. Sensor

It's in the security section of the handbook, which is written out all in lists. I am very big on lists. And by the way, I was told to be as specific as possible in this account, which explains the rambling details. So I am simply complying with orders.

See? I am cooperating.

Which is saying something, because I have major trust issues, except for with people like my friend Flo, who is my ex aunt-in-law. I still don't know exactly how we are related—it's like twice removed by marriage and then even further removed by divorce—but the fact is that Flo has been around my mother and me for all our lives. She called both of us "Kid," probably because she had no kids of her own, so she treated my mother and me like we were her facsimiles thereof. Still, the only reason I trusted her is because she figured out what I was up to two weeks ago and didn't tell anyone. She said she'd never seen anything like it in all her years of flying, which, of course, got her to reminiscing.

"Those were the days to fly, kid," she'd say. "You could smoke and drink Bloody Marys in the galley all day and never have to worry about being Breathalyzed at the end of your shift."

Flo still smokes and drinks Bloody Marys in the galley all day, so I don't know why she was nostalgic about that particular thing. It was the reason she always bid to fly the old Lockheed 1011s, because the galley is located under the cabin in a whole separate area where passengers are not even allowed. She could spend the whole flight down there doing anything she wanted, and she didn't have to answer to anyone—not the passengers, pilots, or even other flight attendants. All she had to do was prepare the carts and send them up in the tiny little elevators, and I usually did that for her. It was part of our deal. That and I was supposed to provide her clean urine samples in case she ever got popped to report for a drug test. So I tried to book myself on as many flights with Flo as I could, because she knew my mother and she knew my situation. Like I said, it did not take her long before she figured out what I was up to after she discovered me in the lost-and-found room of the Detroit employee lounge.

"Kid!" she said, sounding happy and surprised. "What the hell are you doing here?"

She was standing in the doorway with the light coming from behind her, and it illuminated her giant white bun, which made it look like her head was on fire. If you knew Flo, you'd realize why that image is appropriate. As tiny as she is, Flo is never hard to miss. She's a sixty-seven-year-old flight attendant with a white bun on her head as big as a bicycle seat. That bun is the whole reason she ever got hired, she told me, because back in the sixties you had to be at least five-foot-two to be a stewardess, and Flo is technically only five feet and a half-inch tall. The bun, though, put her up over the line, and they didn't start getting really strict about these requirements until the 1980s. I know all the airline history. Just ask me.

"Where's your Rollaboard, kid?" she asked in response to my shocked silence. "Because it looks like you could use a change of clothes."

"It got gate-checked in Los Angeles," I told her.

"You should know better."

I did know better. In fact, I have a whole list of reasons why it's a bad idea to carry luggage at all. Here are the top four:

1. Luggage can obstruct the exit in the event of a plane crash
2. Luggage slows you down between gates during stopovers
3. Luggage can contain a bunch of severed heads (like the abandoned bag of cadaver heads found at O'Hare recently)
4. Even carry-on luggage can be forcibly checked at the door of the plane, never to be seen again

That fourth thing actually happened to me two and a half weeks ago. But to be fair, I should not have booked myself on a Boeing 757, which is a single-aisle jet and therefore has only half the overhead stowage space. A Boeing 757 is now the second worst jet on my list of worst jets to fly nonrevenue. The first on the list is a DC-9, of course, because it's over fifty years old and smells like feet.

But I had hopped the 757 for two reasons: One, I couldn't take the flight to Atlanta because the agent working the gate that day was, in an understatement, suspicious. And two, the 757 was the last flight leaving for Detroit that night, and the Detroit crew lounge is where I know I can still use my mother's badge for access. In Atlanta, for some reason, when I swiped her badge through the security reader and entered her passcode, the door just beeped menacingly and remained locked. It's a good thing everyone's all complacent again and no one ever pays attention to door alarms at airports anymore. They all just assumed it tripped by mistake. So all I had to do was smile and take two steps backward into the crowd and out of suspicion.

That doesn't mean I was *unable* to get into the Atlanta employee lounge, it just means it was not as easy. Like I had to sit in the elevator on the A Concourse until somebody from the employee lounge summoned it from underneath. That way I could ride it down there without having to swipe my mother's badge, and just disembark as though I belonged there. Funny, though, I really did feel like I belonged there.

Again, in Detroit, my mother's badge still worked. And why wouldn't it? She may have been in the nut house, but she was still employed by WorldAir.

The lost-and-found room in the Detroit crew lounge is like a walk-in closet, packed with old suitcases and discarded uniform pieces, but they're still clothes, and flight attendants come in all sizes. I'm a size 4 and some of those pants were too small even for me, while others were big enough to be used as hammocks. That's when Flo busted me, when I was swapping out my old clothes for some new ones.

"C'mon, start talking," she prompted me.

"I ran away," I whispered.

"I gathered that," she said, giving me a hug as, finally, the tears came. Even though her head hardly made it to my elbows, her hugs were still pretty powerful. She locked the door behind her and lit a cigarette that she was not at all supposed to be smoking. Then it occurred to me that the Detroit lost-and-found room was her secret cigarette place. Flo had secret cigarette places in practically every airport that existed, not to mention the airplanes. When it comes to smoking on airplanes she was like a MacGyver all on her own. She kept shower caps in her carry-on bag to slip on the overhead smoke detectors in the 767 lavatories, for one, and she'd blow the smoke right into the sink drain, which has double the suction of a vacuum hose.

I told her what I felt I could without endangering her. Flo is as suspicious of authority and bureaucracy as I am, so thankfully she didn't ask me to turn myself in as a runaway. She knew I'd be better off living in the air than I was at Ash's place. Instead, she made me promise to book myself solely on her flights and stick by her side as much as possible, and when it was not possible, to stay in the employee lounges while keeping in constant contact with her.

"I promise," I told her.

"And this is just for now, kid," she said, extinguishing her cigarette under the toe of her high-heeled black pump, "until we figure something out."

Flo has been working on airplanes since '67, and she used to say she'd retire when her age matched the year she was hired, but that happened this year and now she's all, "I'm never leaving, kid, not until they pry the peanuts from my cold, dead fingers."

I can still feel my heart snap in half after watching her surrender herself to the hijackers. They made her come up from the lower galley of the plane by threatening to kill another passenger unless she gave herself up. I begged her not to do it—especially considering the person they were threatening to kill.

"No matter what we think of him," Flo said, "he doesn't deserve to die at the hands of those animals."

"Oh, Flo," I cried. "We see that differently."

CHAPTER 1

It's been exactly a year to the day—today is my fifteenth birthday, by the way, and I like my cake chocolate with white icing, in case anyone cares—since I started running away, and about two and a half weeks since I've been on the run full time. That's if you want to call me a "runaway," because in order to be a genuine runaway wouldn't your parents need to know you are missing? In my case they had no idea. Since my parents only communicated through me in accordance to various court and/or protection orders, it was easy to let one believe I was with the other.

I would do this for days at a time, hopping planes, wandering airports, and subsisting on pretzel packets and the perishable in-flight food items that you pay for from the cabin snack carts now. Unaccompanied minors are given all that stuff free—sandwiches, salads, fruit and cheese plates—it was better than the boxes of Rice-A-Roni my stepfather kept in his cupboards. He lived like a frat boy minus the pizza crusts, because even leftover pizza would have been better than the ancient staples in his kitchen pantry. I seriously think they were left there by the previous owners.

Ash only fought for shared custody of me for two reasons: One, so he wouldn't have to pay child support, seeing as he had officially adopted me back when I was too young to object, therefore he was beholden to the same responsibilities as a biological father in the same circumstance; and two—and most important—so he could hurt my mother.

When he won, it was probably as big a surprise to him as it was to any of us. Then recently he took it a step further, and the judge—who seemed to think Ash was a saint—recommended he have the title of "primary physical custodian," which the judge of course granted, and now Ash was in charge of all important decisions affecting my life.

It was a stupefying turn of events, and it didn't help at all when my mother attacked Ash's girlfriend Kathy in the hallway outside the Fulton County courtroom during the last contempt hearing, but that's not to say Kathy didn't deserve it. She did. It's just that I've learned that when it comes to divorce and custody cases there are two worlds: the real world, and the bizarro world of family court. Kathy Landry, twenty-nine years old, processed blond hair, pretty in a hardened, face-like-a-frying-pan kinda way, personality of a sea urchin, so skinny you wondered how vital organs could actually fit inside her body, was nowhere near a mother herself (a cactus could die of neglect in her care). In other words, Kathy's character was the perfect combination of emotionless telephone dial tone and soulless rabid badger to help guide Ash through the idiocy of family court.

On the day my mother attacked her, Kathy had provided Ash's attorney with what she referred to as evidence proving my mother was a dangerous alcoholic. This "evidence" was heavily referenced in the guardian ad litem's recommendation, and it consisted of Facebook photos my mom had been tagged in a few weeks prior. It showed her having a good time at Flo's fiftieth birthday party during a layover in Mainz, Germany. I remember hearing about that party. In fact, it lives on in WorldAir legend. The entire crew was so hung over the next day they had to commandeer the emergency personal-oxygen tanks (known as "PO2 bottles" by those in the industry) and take turns huffing pure oxygen in the first-class lavatory. Luckily not a soul was booked in first class on that trip, so that cabin was designated a hangover triage of sorts. The pictures are also legendary, as Flo, to this day, is known for flashing her bra on her birthday.

So all the crew during the layover, including my mother, were flashing their bra-clad chests to the rest of the revelers in the bar. I suppose it looked like they were having fun, especially in the pictures where the ladies took turns kissing the handsome bartender's mouth, but to be truthful they were so drunk that to me they just looked like a group of attractive, bumbling recovering stroke victims. I'm betting more fun was had in remembering the event than in the actual experiencing of it, because today Flo is sixty-seven years old.

Yes, you heard me right. Those pictures were taken over seventeen years ago, soon after my mother had been hired on as a flight attendant. Not only were they depicting an event that occurred years before I was born, but before she ever met Ash Manning, or even my father. In the real world those pictures would have had no bearing whatsoever on judging a person's parenting abilities. But remember, family court doesn't live in the real world.

In family court those pictures were validated by the date reflected on them—the date they had been uploaded to the Facebook account—and that date was just a few weeks prior to the contempt hearing, and most of the time, as in this case, the judge doesn't even *see* the pictures. His decisions are based on the guardian ad litem's report, and the report in this case stated, verbatim (I know this because I read it), "Facebook photos dated during Mother's custodial time show her highly inebriated and engaging in acts of public indecency." See? See how it's a technically accurate statement but at the same time a big, crappy, soul-sucking lie? *That's* what family court is like.

Again, I don't blame my mother for attacking Kathy. Kathy Landry is a she-beast and a succubus. Whenever I'm around her she talks about me as though I'm not there, referring to me as "The Child," as in, "It would serve the court for you to e-mail your ex-wife a list of suggested summer camps, Ash. That way it would appear as though you take an interest in The Child's extracurricular activity."

I would not have known about the attack if not for the fact that it became the most popular link on the local news website and got splattered all over everybody's Twitter feeds. "WorldAir Flight Attendant Arrested for Assault and Terroristic Threats," the headline read. It was impossible not to click on that.

I'm attaching for you my copy of the news thread:

WorldAir Flight Attendant Arrested for Assault and Terroristic Threats

January 15, 2013—Elizabeth Manning, 39, a flight attendant for WorldAir, was arrested this afternoon and charged with assault for allegedly attacking Kathy Landry, 29, a corporate attorney for WorldAir. The alleged assault occurred at 3:15 P.M. outside the chambers of Judge Jonathan Cheevers of the Fulton County family court. A security alarm was sounded, prompting police to flood the fifth floor of the Fulton County courthouse, subsequently drawing weapons on Manning, who held Landry in a headlock and "looked about to break her in half," recounted bystander Leroy Dunst.

"This tall lady here grabbed that skinny lady there," he said, indicating Manning and Landry, respectively, "and went about trying to snap her like a chicken bone. Good the police got here, she mighta coulda done it."

Manning eventually released Landry amid a barrage of verbal threats, which prompted police into a further investigation of her behavior, said Officer Barkley Jefferson, the Atlanta Police Department's public information officer. "We discovered some disturbing comments recently posted to Ms. Manning's Facebook account," he added. "I'm not authorized to divulge anything beyond that, except to say Ms. Manning is also under investigation by the FBI for terroristic threats." Currently Manning is being held without bail at an undisclosed Fulton County correctional facility.

My mother's mug shot, included in later editions of the story, was wondrous. Somehow her makeup remained impeccable while her long hair, dyed a sunkissed gold that almost perfectly matched the hair of her youth (and my own natural color), must have been knocked out of its updo. The result was an unexpected glamorous cascade that fell far below the frame of her inmate placard. Her large green eyes sparkled with a mirth I knew meant trouble, and her lips were twisted into a curious half smile. Thinking back, I bet she was going for a smirk, but smirking was new to her. In any event, my mother's mug shot was so beautiful she could have used it as a profile picture on an Internet dating site. Ironic, really, since she'd sworn off dating for life.

After that incident, my mother's attorney arranged for her to be admitted to a psychiatric facility to be treated for an emotional breakdown. "It doesn't mean she's crazy, kid," Flo tried to comfort me. "It's a tactic just like any other. She can't get fired while she's on family medical leave, and she can't get prosecuted for the assault as long as she's receiving treatment for a mental breakdown."

Because her attorney was able to place my mother in a facility that accepted WorldAir insurance under the Family Medical Leave act, it meant Ash couldn't track her down. She had long since put in the request to have her employee information restricted so that nobody—especially Ash—could gain access to it unless, like me, they had her username and password.

And, thank God, my mother's attorney was able to get the "terroristic threats" charge dropped from the docket. My mother herself had not posted any disturbing comments on her Facebook page. It turned out that, against my express instructions, she had no privacy settings whatsoever on her Facebook account, and the second the security clip of her attacking Kathy went viral it unleashed a spike of psycho postings on my mother's page that she had nothing to do with. Still, though, it's out there. Now when you do a Google search of my mother's name, her mug shot and "terroristic threats" dominate the first page of search results, not to mention "psychiatric evaluation."

"At least she can't get fired," Flo reassured me. "The nut house was a genius move, really. It puts everything in a holding pattern until we can figure out a new battle plan."

Holding pattern. That phrase has perfectly described my life ever since. I have no cell phone (that's considered an "important decision affecting my life," so Ash naturally said no), so I communicated with my mother via Skype using my iPad, but only when I had access to a strong WiFi Internet signal, which did not include Ash's condo. My mother tried to laughingly refer to her time in the nut house as her "spa getaway," and told me she loves me. I love her, too, but it was hard not to be mad at her. Don't get me wrong; I understand the odds were stacked against her, and that Ash was underhanded and used his girlfriend as a stick to stir the big cauldron of crazy that is family court. I understood that none of this was fair.

But while I was growing up my mother always told me, "Don't freak out. *Figure* it out." Like when I was eleven and my troll of a second cousin used to intercept me at family picnics to stomp on my toes because my feet were "as big as surfboards" and always got in her way. I used to freak out and cry, to no avail. Then my mother bought me a pair of steel-toed Doc Martens. Troll Cousin could stomp on my toes until her foot fell off and I wouldn't feel a thing. And that steel toe left a helluva bruise on her shin, too.

So I feel like my mother broke her own rule. She should have figured out how to navigate the landscape of family court, how to combat the enemy. I know she was facing an unfair fight, but since when was life fair? Don't freak out. *Figure* it out.

CHAPTER 2

It was right after the divorce when Ash decided to transfer himself to LAX, thus commencing the necessity for me to fly there unaccompanied every other week in order to fulfill the custodial order. More than half the time Ash would forget to pick me up at the airport, and I'd have to catch a ride with one of the sympathetic gate agents. Eventually Ash took it for granted that I'd appear on my own. I got to know many of the gate agents who worked the ATL and LAX routes, because airline employees have their patterns, and I'm good at discerning patterns.

For example, Tyreese Washington is my favorite gate agent out of ATL, because he's a short man with a big personality. When he makes announcements over the PA he sounds like a carnival barker. When it was time to issue my seat assignment, he'd wink at me and announce, "Step right up, beautiful little lady." I started bringing him coffee from the employee cafeteria ("Three creams, no sugar—you're all the sweetness I need"), and sometimes he let me sit by the dot matrix printer behind the gate so I could pull the departure report when it emerged, and twice he even let me deliver the departure report to the coordinator at the end of the jetway.

Out of LAX I liked Jalyce Johnson, because she'd often given me a ride to Ash's place after noticing I'd been abandoned at the gate. If I were flying unaccompanied-minor as a revenue passenger, the airline would have dispatched an agent to be at my side until my parent or guardian arrived. But because I am the progeny of WorldAir's own personnel—which, again, means I fly free (or "nonrevenue")—the airline is absolved of that responsibility . . . or, more accurately, that responsibility gets transferred to the minor nonrevenue's employee parents, and the airline stays out of it.

The first time Jalyce gave me a ride was when she saw me walking down Sepulveda Boulevard and pulled over. She had even remembered my name from the passenger manifest, and I remembered her because of her hair, which was ice-white and cut in a mod pixie style. She also wore oversized tortoiseshell eyeglasses. The look really worked for her. "Get in. This is no place for a young lady to be walking around alone," she admonished me. "Right over there is where the Hillside Stranglers nabbed one of their victims." She pointed to the bus stop where I had actually been headed. "Do you know who the Hillside Stranglers were?"

"Who doesn't?" I said as I buckled my seatbelt. As a kid, watching true-crime television was considered mother-daughter bonding time. The Hillside Stranglers were an uncle and nephew team of exceptionally foul-hearted serial killers who prowled the Los Angeles area during the seventies, torturing their victims, sometimes for days at a time, and then brazenly dumping their desecrated bodies in open areas like hillsides and roadsides. Their method of operation was to descend on a girl, show her a fake police badge and demand she come with them to their car. Almost all their victims complied without question. "The Hillside Stranglers," I went on, "are the reason why, if ever a man shows me a police badge and says I have to leave with him, I'm supposed to kick him in the crotch and run away."

"Who told you that?"

"My mom."

"Your mom is a smart lady."

"We see that differently."

Jalyce let that pass and asked me where I was headed. I told her and she whistled softly. "Manhattan Beach," she said. "Your dad a pilot?"

"He's not my real dad, and yes, he's a pilot," I explained, adding a run-down of my crazy custodial situation.

"You mean he's not even related to you and he won legal custody?" she asked. "How does that happen? Did your mom show up with hypodermic needles hanging out of her arms or something?"

"No, that's just it, she's a great mom, if you subtract the fact that she married a controlling borderline sociopath," I answered. I had yet to hack into my mother's e-mail and read all the court documents, so like everyone else I assumed she must have done something terrible to deserve losing me. "Beats me what happened."

"Was there a guardian ad litem assigned to your case?" she asked.

"I don't know. What's a guardian ad litem?"

And that is how I learned about GALs. Jalyce had a large layman's knowledge about the intricacies of family law because her "baby daddy" routinely took her to court with crazy ploys to lessen his child support payments, and she lent a sympathetic ear to my situation. After that day I always tried to book myself on flights that left from her gate. She always let me board the plane while the ground crew was still cleaning the cabin. I liked to help by gathering the newspapers and other bulky trash and piling it all in one place for them, like in a forward seat next to the exit.

To be truthful, I wasn't just being benevolent by helping them—people leave the most amazing things behind in their seats. Like last year I scored a portable DVD player along with all seven seasons of *MacGyver*. Lately it was almost all I had for entertainment, except for the books I pick up while helping the ground crew clean the cabin. But let me tell you, I have serious concerns about the state of today's bestseller list. The last couple of books I read were epic period romances where the heroine gets raped a hundred times and then ends up all in love with the guy who totally treated her the crappiest. No, thank you.

So I've started being more picky about reading the books I find, which meant my amusement got restricted to *MacGyver* episodes and the WiFi signal outside the Flight Club lounges or on board the airplanes, because unaccompanied minors get free Internet if they ask for it. All the flight attendant has to do is give you her access code. But in-flight WiFi won't let you stream video. So I'd use that time to complete my class assignments in order to keep my virtual high-school teachers from marking me truant, or whatever they do if you don't complete your online assignments. I seriously have no idea what they do in that event.

All I know is that when Officer Ned Rockwell threatened to turn me in for truancy, I knew his threats were empty. I was current in my studies and had nothing to fear in that regard. I tried explaining it to him on our first flight together, but he got that glazed look older people get when you talk technology with them. I even had to show him how to download apps on his iPad so we could play *Neuroshima Hex!* together to pass the time.

In all, I've encountered Officer Rockwell three times. Law enforcement officers (or LEOs, as they are known on the departure reports) can board the plane before everybody else, the same as unaccompanied minors, and the gate agents like to sit them near each other. LEOs can also be part of the briefing process with the pilots and cabin crew if they choose, since often they are escorting prisoners and carrying firearms, like air marshals.

Air marshals, though, and I'm sure you know this, don't alert anyone to their presence. I hear that rule got started because air marshals kept getting asked to intervene with petty disturbances, like when passengers bitch too loudly about not getting their meal choice—or, lately, any meal at all—and, you know, air marshals aren't supposed to handle that; flight attendants are supposed to handle that.

But—and this is just my opinion—if air marshals don't want to alert us to their presence, you should tell them to stop wearing Hawaiian shirts. Everyone knows that the universal "regular guy" uniform for air marshals is a Hawaiian shirt, jeans, and tennis shoes, even for the *female* ones. And they always order a cocktail, but don't drink it. That is seriously common knowledge, and they aren't fooling anyone. Just my two cents, which should be of some value—don't you think?—considering what happened to the air marshal on today's flight. But I digress.

LEOs also have a somewhat common look, too. For example, they usually wear Dockers and a polo shirt under a sports jacket they never remove, no matter how hot it gets in the plane. This is because of the gun they're packing. So LEOs are easy to spot, too, but they aren't supposed to be traveling incognito, so I have no criticism regarding their attire.

Officer Rockwell and I have often encountered each other in the airport concourse, but he has only been on two of my flights. The first time was a few months ago when he was escorting a car thief who had been arrested in Georgia and then extradited to California. The prisoner was handcuffed, and sat in the window seat. He was skinny, with dirty blond dreadlocks pulled back in a thick ponytail, dressed in jeans and a T-shirt that said Stop Staring at My Tits!, which I thought was pretty funny. (If I tried to wear that on the plane I'd be turned back at the gate, regardless of the fact that I hardly have anything to stare at.) Officer Rockwell took the seat next to him on the aisle, which put him right across the aisle from me. We were the only passengers on the plane so far, and Officer Rockwell must have noticed the eager expression on my face because he nodded hello. I took that as permission to incessantly grill him with questions throughout the rest of boarding and taxi:

"What happens if he escapes?"

"What happens if he has to go to the lavatory? Do you have to release his handcuffs?"

"What happens if there is an 'unanticipated landing'? Do you have to release his handcuffs?"

"What happens if there is a rapid decompression and he can't reach his mask? Are you gonna let him suffocate?"

"What happens if there's an emergency landing and the cabin fills with smoke? How is he gonna feel his way out of the fuselage?"

"What happens if the escape chutes are deployed? How is he gonna slide down them all handcuffed like he is?"

Officer Rockwell tried to ignore me, but good luck with that on a five-hour flight. "Kid," he finally hissed. "Shut the hell up. You're freaking us all out."

I looked around and saw that he was right. It turned out people are not enthusiastic about listening to all the ways a flight can go wrong while you're sitting on the tarmac about to take off. Already three of the people surrounding us had broken federal regulation and put their earphones back on. Personally, I think it's relaxing to go through all possible disaster scenarios in my head as we taxi out. I have a list, of course. It helps calm me down. My friend Malcolm is the same way. I really don't get why it doesn't work for everyone.

"Don't use profanity," I told him. "I'm impressionable."

"'Hell' is not a profane word," he corrected me. "And if you're so impressionable, where the hell are your parents?"

"I'm flying unaccompanied. I do it all the time."

"Why?"

"Because my parents are divorced and they live across the country from each other. They both work for the airline so I fly free. My custody schedule is week on/week off."

"What does that mean?" he asked, furrowing his brow. If I didn't know better, I could have sworn he was a little nervous about flying. It probably did not help that he was about a hundred feet tall ("six-five," he later corrected me), and his knees were practically bundled under his chin in order for him to fit in the economy seats. It's a good thing he got to wear regular clothes and not his uniform.

"This is an MD-88," I said, evading his question.

"I know that." He took the safety card out of the seat pocket in front of him and waved it at me curtly. This prompted his prisoner to take out his own safety card and study it like it was a total treasure map.

"I'm just saying, because the economy-class seats are only seventeen inches wide," I yammered. "Do you wanna know what's bigger than seventeen inches?"

"I'm sure there are a lot of things bigger than seventeen inches," he drolled.

"The average seat of a baby stroller is nineteen inches wide. Can you believe that? These seats are two inches narrower than the seat of a baby stroller."

Officer Ned closed his eyes slowly and kept his head facing forward. He was a light-skinned African American with freckles and eyes the color of caramel. He wore his hair close-cropped and was probably in his early forties, which made his goatee kind of unfortunate. He had a space between his two front teeth that made him look more approachable that he probably liked. Plus he looked kind of weary, so maybe he could have been younger. I don't know why I wanted to talk to him so much. Like I said, I have major trust issues. But I read in one of my mother's books that it's important to have a "support system" in place when you go through a crisis. And if you ask me I was going through a crisis right then. Suffice it to say that of the few friends I had, almost all of them were airline personnel. Malcolm was my only friend my age, but Malcolm wasn't there that day. So I thought it would serve my purpose to create a new ally to "strengthen my support system," like the book said to do.

And maybe it was the weariness of his face that drew me to Officer Ned, because I related to that. Also, I knew I'd probably see him again. You don't fly as much as I do without recognizing the potential for repeat run-ins. Patterns, remember? And since he was a LEO, I figured it would be best to get on his good side.

The cuffed criminal next to him kept trying to order tequila from the beverage cart, and it was becoming an old joke. Officer Ned had a lot less tolerance for him than he did for me.

"So what does week on/week off mean? You never told me," he said to me after a while. The MD-88 had no onboard entertainment system, not even any music in the armrest; it was just a matter of time before he became desperate enough for distraction to talk to me.

I turned to him eagerly, happy to begin cracking his hardened defenses, although I was *not* so eager to talk about my ridiculous parental situation. He struck me as someone who would require very little input to surmise that I was on the run. But it looked like he wasn't really listening, anyway, so I decided to open up a little—give and take.

"It means that I spend one week with one parent and the next week with the other, and so on and so on," I answered.

"All year long?" he asked incredulously. So he was listening after all.

"Yeah, it's not the best of situations," I said.

"And your parents live across the country from each other?" He was still incredulous. I was used to it. Non-airline people always get their cockles in a bundle about our lifestyles. Like my mother once flew me to Rome because we were out of Parmesan cheese. People act like this is child abuse or something. It's not. It's awesome.

But that's different from this situation—this back-and-forth cross-country custody—*this* was abusive, or at the very least negligent. The last thing this custodial schedule did was "put my welfare at a precedent," which is a legal phrase I kept coming across when I hacked into my mother's e-mail account and read all the court documents her attorney had sent her. It was used in reference to the life decisions my mother and Ash had made, and whether those decisions placed me at a priority. I thought it was ironic, because I felt this custodial schedule put my welfare nowhere near anyone's precedent. For example, I've sat next to perverts who watch porn on their iPads all flight, Pentecostal religious freaks who outlined my damnation for hours on end, a drunk who befouled himself in his sleep, petty thieves who tried to steal my neck pillow and my *Mac-Gyver* DVDs, one man who I swear had hepatitis, a woman who breastfed her eight-year-old, *Corey* freakin' *Feldman*, and right now I was sitting less than three feet away from a handcuffed criminal, and even closer to a loaded gun.

"What about school?" Officer Ned asked. "I have half a mind to report you for truancy."

"I study at an online academy."

"So you're homeschooled?"

"No, it's part of the Atlanta public school system, I just do everything online. I only have to log in for a few hours a week as long as I complete all my assignments." The next one due, I told him, was a thousand-word composition on the five people I admire the most. "Isn't that corny?" I asked. He did not answer.

I'd recently read in a discarded *Atlanta Business Chronicle* that the Atlanta online school option arose as a response to the fact that the state of Georgia stands about five spots below slug farts when it comes to education in our country, while at the same time becoming one of the fastest growing business markets. So when an influx of professionals moved to Atlanta, they didn't want to enroll their kids in the existing schools that regularly failed the mandated competency requirements, so *boom!*, instant online academy. Problem solved for everybody but kids like me, because now parents were totally unobligated to maintain a stable location; now they could just divorce and move anywhere, willy-nilly, placing all the onus on the kid to be flexible. Case in point: Ash and Elizabeth Manning. I was paraphrasing and surmising, and I admit I was jaded about this subject, so maybe my experience wasn't universal.

"Wow," Officer Ned said, backing away from me a bit. *I really need to work on my social skills*, I thought. It's not a good sign when someone instinctively inches closer to a known criminal after you go off on a little rant.

"So what about you?" I chirped. Perkiness was new to me, but I did my best.

"Typical story," he sulked, sipping his water.

"Did you ever kill anybody?"

"Not today," he said dryly. "Yet."

"Har har," I said, watching him put the plastic cup to his lips. I could have sworn he did it to conceal a smile beginning to curl at his lips. *My ploy is working*, I thought, *I'm charming*.

"My name is April," I told him. "What's yours?"

"Officer Edward Rockwell," he said, placing emphasis on the word "officer." After a pregnant pause he added, "But you can call me Officer Ned."

"Awesome," I said. "So, really, Officer Ned, seriously, did you ever kill anyone? And what caliber is the gun you're packing? And do you wanna see how I can escape from handcuffs?"

"Please," he said, rubbing his temples, "be quiet."

Then the captain announced our final approach. The passengers were told to put their seatbacks forward and tray tables upright to prepare for landing, and the flight attendants made their way down the aisle to point out bags that needed to be stowed. Officer Ned stood to put his carry-on in the compartment above him, and his prisoner, who'd been sleeping open-mouthed and fogging up the cabin with his halitosis hoosegow breath most of the flight, suddenly popped up and claimed to be in dire need of a toilet. I guess it was understandable, since he'd been boxed in for five hours.

"Seriously, man," he pleaded, "my gut is percolating like a pressure cooker. If you don't let me go now, it's not gonna be pretty."

Truthfully, I was hoping Officer Ned would let him go to the lav, because he had a complexion the color of concrete and looked to be experiencing drug withdrawals. In the flight attendant manual there's a section on this in the chapter on first aid, and I was worried this guy would start spewing out of every orifice like a busted beer keg. Officer Ned must have had the same thought, because he stepped aside and let the prisoner, still handcuffed, run to the rear of the plane just as the wheels touched the tarmac.

The flight attendant in the rear jumpseat looked really put out for having to unstrap himself and stand in order to fold up his seat so the prisoner could open the door of the lavatory. Rather than reassume his jumpseat, the flight attendant moved into the pocket galley a few rows up and closed the curtain so he could finish texting in peace. This left the flight attendant at midcabin to admonish everyone else to stay seated, because often when one person jumps up on taxi everyone else takes it as a cue to follow suit.

"Ladies and gentlemen, the plane is still on an active taxi," she announced. "Please stay seated until the aircraft has come to a complete stop and the captain has turned off the fasten-seatbelt sign." Once she finished her announcement she immediately re-engrossed herself in the tabloid opened on her lap, a total violation of federal regulations, by the way.

I kept my eyes expectantly on Officer Ned.

"What?" he finally asked.

"You know there's a tailcone exit on this plane, don't you?" I said.

"Really? Well, I doubt my prisoner can open it," he chuckled.

"It tells you how to open it right here in the safety card," I told him. I pulled the card out of my seat pocket and unfolded it. "Right here," I pointed. "And there's no flight attendant manning the back of the plane right now."

When I say Officer Ned moved in a flash, I am not exaggerating. It was like, *whoosh!*, and he was halfway to the back just as the prisoner opened the aft door, which the flight attendant had already disarmed—another *total* FAA violation, seeing as how the plane had not come to a complete stop yet. Because of this the tailcone did not drop and deploy the slide, as it would have if it was armed like it should have been. What happened instead was worse.

I got up and followed right behind, because I did not want to miss this. When you open the tailcone exit of an MD-88 in the disarmed position, it enables you to lower the aft staircase, the one reserved for the ground crew so they can enter the plane from the back and begin cleaning the cabin before the passengers are even finished disembarking through the front door.

In this case, the prisoner, who had unlocked his handcuffs (not surprising, since there are hundreds of tutorials on YouTube showing you exactly how), was already at the end of the catwalk along the interior of the tailcone by the time Officer Ned dove through the back door and missed the man's ankles by about a nano-inch. The other passengers had jumped up from their seats, thinking all the activity meant it was okay to start gathering their carry-ons and lumber toward the exit, oblivious to the fact that one, the plane was still moving, and two, anything was wrong. The flight attendant at midcabin, equally oblivious, kept repeating her PA admonishment for everyone to remain seated or she'd have to tell the captain to stop the plane on the tarmac, which would actually have been a good thing to do, but she never did it.

The attendant who should have been manning the aft door was still holed up in the side galley. He did not so much as peek through the curtain, not even when the fire started.

Because it turns out that when you drag a metal staircase along asphalt behind an airplane in the hot California sun, it causes sparks. And sparks cause fires. Luckily I'd grabbed the Halon extinguisher from the bracket behind the last seat on my way back there. I didn't expect to use it to actually put out a fire, because a Halon extinguisher happens to be a great weapon in case you need to throw it at the head of an escaping car thief, but then the sparks ignited the brake pad on one of the landing gears, and, well, there was nothing for it but to pull the pin on the extinguisher and begin spraying it in a fan formation as the flight attendant manual instructs.

Before the smoke obstructed my view, I saw Officer Ned overtake his prisoner right as he was about to reach the chain-link fence along the runway. It was a pretty impressive sight, considering the head start the thief had on him. But Officer Ned has legs like rockets, he really does. I'm glad he's one of my few friends.

Regarding the fire, all I had to do was pull the inflation handle of the escape slide. Once it deployed and came in contact with the fire, which hadn't grown that big (it takes ninety seconds for a fire to grow out of control), the slide popped and the ensuing burst of air extinguished the flames. I snuffed any residual flames with the extinguisher. By then we'd reached the gate and the jetway was already in place. Later Flo told me that the pilots never even knew anything went wrong other than the incessant beeping on their flight panel indicating an open aft door, which they ignored, and the flight attendants remained oblivious as well, until all the passengers had disembarked and they noticed a charred tailcone exit at the back of the plane.

The tower did notice the commotion, though—it would have been hard for them not to—and so had dispatched a swarm of emergency personnel. FAA officials and airport security had started to descend upon the jetway, along with airline representatives clutching in-flight incident forms for people to fill out, but I slipped by them unnoticed.

I'm just an unaccompanied minor. What do I know.

CHAPTER 3

Ash's place is a dismally furnished one-bedroom condo where he expected me to sleep on patio cushions he put on the floor of his laundry room. It's located in Manhattan Beach, a neighborhood near LAX that is super popular with newly divorced airline pilots. They move there thinking they're part of this hip-surfer-bikini community, when really it's mostly middle-aged divorced old crust buckets like Ash all trying to suck the youth out of the sand or something. It's pretty pathetic, and I hate it.

Ash's girlfriend Kathy doesn't even live in Manhattan Beach. She lives in Carlsbad, which is about two hours south of LAX and one of the reasons Ash is never home. Lately I'd spent entire custodial periods at his place without laying eyes on him, which was fine with me. He would usually call his landline, though, to make sure I'd arrived. Because if I hadn't it meant my mother hadn't followed the judge's order, and he could drag her back into court again. Ash had a maddening advantage over my mother considering his girlfriend was an attorney and every bit as empty-hearted as he was.

But what made it all the more maddening was that it was clear Ash didn't want me around. I'm not surmising here; he told me so all the time.

"Can you get lost? Kathy's coming over and she doesn't like you lurking around," he'd say as he stood in front of the mirror in the foyer, running his fingers through his thinning hair to distribute the mousse evenly. I didn't get why women found him attractive. I mean, sure, he had the blond hair and blue eyes and he was kind of tall and he'd held up okay physically for being forty-nine, but he was vain and mean and there was that black, sucking sinkhole in his chest where his heart should be. Personally I wondered how his romantic prospects got around that.

"Move it!" he hissed at me.

"My absolute pleasure, *Dad*," I hissed back. At this point I'd usually grab my things and catch the bus to the airport to sneak into the employee lounge to eat the free snacks they sometimes put out for the crew. All I had to do to get past security was list myself on a flight, print the boarding voucher and stand next to a big family in the security line so the TSA agent would assume I was with them. As long as I stayed in the concourses on the other side of security, I never had to show my passport again. I could literally fly all over the country without going through another checkpoint.

That's why checked baggage has been such a downside since I've been disappeared for the past three weeks. Baggage claim is outside the security checkpoint. To retrieve a bag would have meant leaving the concourse and then re-entering through security. I rarely chanced it. About six weeks ago when I was just a part-time runaway, before I disappeared, I was in a hurry and tried to simply go through security on my own without piggybacking on a big family. I'd done it a few times before without incident; I showed them my passport and they must have just assumed I was over eighteen. But that day I got popped by a TSA agent who, judging from her appearance, I could have sworn would have been a complete cakewalk.

"Young lady, where is your escort?" she asked me sternly. I knew I was in trouble the second she called me "young lady." She wore her hair in a mass of long cornrows supplemented by hot-pink extensions all bunched up and sprouting from the top of her head like an erupting volcano. She eyed me levelly over the top of purple-and-red-framed reading glasses.

"My mom has gone through already. I'm just trying to catch up with her," I answered. I was friendly and confident and looked her in the eye. I had practiced this.

"Well, we can't let you through security unless you're being escorted by a parent or guardian," she said humorlessly. *Dang*, I thought, *she must have kids of her own.* Mothers are the hardest to fool.

"My mom's probably just trying to get rid of me," I joked.

"Um-hm." She sounded not at all like she was buying my act, which was saying something, because my act was pretty good. Instead she eyed me like a shoplifter, unhooked her walkie-talkie, and spoke into it, directing her colleague to "monitor" me until they could find my mother. I spent the next forty minutes sitting next to the surveillance podium while various TSA agents took fruitless turns paging my mother over the airport PA system.

Then—thank God!—I saw Officer Ned making his way to the head of the line. He must have been on his way back from escorting another prisoner, because I could tell he was wearing his gun holster even though he was alone. He looked as irritated with the slow-moving crowd as he must have looked with the criminal he'd ferried around earlier—and as he customarily did with me, come to think of it—but that didn't stop me from calling out to him.

"Officer Ned, hi! Over here! Officer Ned!" The other TSA agents were a little startled by my hollering, but thankfully

Volcano Head had gone on a break, so without her critical eye on me I felt more free to call attention to myself. "Here! Hi, Officer Ned!" I hooted.

He finally heard me and lifted his head to scan the crowd like he was searching for someone who'd made an offensive remark. *This guy needs to cheer up*, I thought. When he caught sight of me he rolled his eyes and shook his head as though my appearance in his life right then was the rotten cherry on top of the crap sundae that had been his afternoon. Undeterred, I smiled excitedly and added jumping to my arm waving. Eventually, after struggling back into his black motorcycle boots (who wears motorcycle boots through a *TSA scan?*), he lumbered over to me while refastening the watch he'd removed for the security scan. His badge hung on his belt, half visible beneath the waistband of his lightweight bomber jacket, a departure from the usual LEO suit jacket.

"What is wrong with you, April? You can't be yelling out my name. I'm supposed to be incognito," he said.

"False," I answered. I was the wrong person for him to try to con, because I knew that plainclothed LEOs are not expected to travel undercover. "You're just saying that so people won't bother you."

"Exactly."

He nodded his acknowledgement to the TSA officer in the podium at my side, who gave him the invisible law-enforcement brotherhood handshake and asked, "Are you here to escort this young lady to her gate? Her mother isn't answering any of our pages."

"Yes, that's exactly right," I interjected. "I'll be fine now, thanks for your help. Officer Rockwell can take me to my gate. I'm sure my mother's there waiting for me. Shall we go, Officer Rockwell?" I grabbed my backpack, hooked my arm through his elbow and half-dragged him onto the concourse.

When we got to a safe distance from the security area he dug in his heels and gently yanked his arm away. "What the hell's going on here?"

"By the way, you're *welcome*," I teased him.

"I'm welcome for *what*?"

"For saving your butt when that prisoner tried to escape." I nudged him playfully, but Officer Ned was about as playful as a porcupine. Still, his face softened with reluctant appreciation.

"Thank you," he sighed. "*Now* tell me what the hell is going on here."

"You heard the TSA agent," I lied. "I got separated from my mother and she didn't hear their pages, which, you know, can you blame her?" I cupped my hands behind my ears to indicate the fact that the airport PA system sounded as clear as a ham radio during a hurricane. "I probably would have been there forever if you hadn't come along. Thanks!"

"Where are you flying? I'm taking you to your gate and meeting your mother."

"I'm catching flight 1420 to Atlanta," I said.

"No, you're not." He eyed me intently. "That flight was canceled."

"Well, then we're just gonna take the next flight."

"No, you're not," he said again. He was really starting to bother me. "All flights to Atlanta are canceled. Haven't you been listening to the announcements?"

"Who can hear the announcements?" I asked. It was a reasonable question. "Nobody can hear anything through these speakers." Later I found out that an overloaded electrical transformer had blown up beneath the D Concourse at Hartsfield and closed down the entire airport for the rest of the night. It was the first time in the history of forever that anything like that had happened, and wouldn't you know, it occurred just as I was trying to lie my butt off to a police officer.

"What's your mother's cell phone number?" Officer Ned flipped open his phone expectantly.

I didn't skip a beat. "The TSA agents already tried calling her." My eyes were wide with honesty. "But her phone is dead."

Officer Ned snapped his phone shut impatiently. He took a card from his breast pocket. "I'm starting to find it a little hard to believe that your mother hasn't called the police and enlisted a SWAT team to try and find you." He handed me the card. "Do you see what it says there? I am an officer of the law. I will talk to your mother, do you understand? Right now. Take me to her this second. Or," he continued, "you can just cut the crap and tell me what's going on here, April."

"Okay, fine." I took a deep breath and let it out with an air of dramatic dejection. "I'll tell you everything. First I have to pee, though. Can I please go pee? There're no bathroom breaks when you're practically held prisoner at security."

You really can't blame Officer Ned for losing me after that. First, I knew from experience that begging to use the bathroom was an effective ruse with him, and second, how was he to know that the door to the crew lounge was down the same hallway that led to the concourse restrooms? Or that I could gain access through that door, descend the stairs, and disappear into the busy lower region of the airport?

Escape like this was one of the benefits that came with impersonating my mother. And WorldAir was such a large corporation that any discrepancies juxtaposing her pass travel against her nut house commitment would not be discovered for months, possibly even years, if ever. For example, it had been eleven years since the death of my real father, and we still received his empty pay stub in the mail every month. The industry machine moves very slowly in this regard, so I felt secure in using her badge to camp in the crew lounges and even to book myself in the jumpseat sometimes, since I'm five-nine, which is tall for a fifteen-year-old, and when I spatula makeup on my face and wear my hair in a twist, I can pass for her now that they don't put birthdates on the badges anymore.

That night, once I was certain I'd ditched Officer Ned, I moseyed over to the employee cafeteria and used my mother's badge to buy a "payroll-deduct" hamburger, finished all of my homework—barring the composition on the five people I admire the most; I was having a hard time with that one (I wonder why)—and spent the night in one of the comfortable La-Z-Boys clustered in a dark corner for flight attendants to use when they need to catch some snores between trips. I would have slept better if not for a coworker (I consider them coworkers), who noisily masticated a big bag of microwave popcorn all night. Seriously, I wanted to swat it out of her hands like how they showed us to do to weapon-wielding assailants in the flight attendant self-defense training video.

Swat it to the ground! I kept thinking. It was such a satisfying mental image, all the popcorn flying in the air. *Swat it to the ground!* I grinned and attached my earphones to my charging portable DVD player. I was on episode sixty-five of *MacGyver*, "The Secret of Parker House," in which MacGyver accompanies his friend Penny Parker (played by Teri Hatcher) to an old house she inherited from her aunt, but suspects foul play when the house appears to be haunted. I fell asleep just as he was improvising a torpedo using a pipe and an old boilerplate.

The next morning I booked myself on the first flight to Atlanta as a nonrevenue employee using my mother's badge, because the standby list was a mile long due to all the cancellations from the night before. By listing myself as a jump-seating flight attendant instead of an unaccompanied minor, I could at least grab a jump-seat if no passenger seats were left.

It was just my luck that Officer Ned was standing by for the same flight. I tried to avoid him, but he must have been on the lookout for me. When he caught sight of me he looked furious, but also, I could have sworn, a little relieved as well.

"Officer Ned!" I exclaimed, figuring I might as well play up our encounter. I rushed over and threw my arms around him. He stiffened with surprise, but after a second he patted my shoulder awkwardly. "I've been looking everywhere for you!" I cried. The people around us began to gaze fondly upon our reunion.

Officer Ned detangled himself and held me at arm's length. "All right, April." He nodded skeptically. "One more time, where's your mother?"

"She's already on board," I lied.

"Really? They haven't even begun the boarding process!" He was angry now.

I hesitated for exactly one second before answering him. "Ah, she's working the flight. All the cancellations from yesterday really screwed up flight attendant scheduling."

"Right." He rolled his eyes.

"Seriously, she volunteered to work the flight so the plane could meet minimum staffing requirements. I'll introduce you when you get on board, I swear."

"Is that so? Well, we'll just wait here until they call our names and board the plane together, then."

"Great, okay! Ah, did you hear that announcement earlier?"

"What announcement?"

"They announced my name. I must have been cleared to board. Haven't they called your name?"

"I did not hear any announcement."

There had been no announcement, but as a jumpseat passenger I didn't need one. I was expected to board before everyone else in order to identify myself to the cabin and cockpit crews.

Officer Ned walked me over to the flustered gate agent. "Excuse me!" he called loudly. I winced. Gate agents hate that. "I said, excuse me!"

The agent smacked her pen on the counter and turned to him sharply. "Yes?"

"Is this young lady cleared to board?"

I'd shown her my badge earlier when I'd filled out the jumpseat slip, so she simply waved her hand dismissively and said, "Yes, of course."

"Fine," Officer Ned said to me. "Get on the plane. At least I'll know where you are."

I gave him another unexpected hug goodbye. It was mostly out of appreciation for having someone give a crap about me for once, but also because I wanted to add his badge to the handcuffs I'd pickpocketed off him earlier. It would be a while before he noticed them missing, I thought, and I had a feeling they might come in handy for me later.

"I'll be on board myself as soon as I get my seat assigned," he called to me as I walked down the jetway.

As I predicted, Officer Ned did not get a seat for that flight, or the next, or the next. I looked up the standby lists later to see that it had taken eleven hours for all the displaced full-fare standby passengers to finally make it to their final destinations.

So I confidently stepped onto the aircraft, nodded hello to the cabin crew, and gratefully claimed one of the open jumpseats near the aft lavatories. This was a Lockheed L-1011, Flo's favorite airplane. Personally, I'd put this plane near the bottom of my own list because it's forty-two years old and reminds me of a dilapidated motor home with wings, not to mention that it's one of the few models of planes left that isn't updated to offer onboard WiFi. But I knew that if I booked an L-1011 flight I had a chance Flo would be working it, and she liked to sneak me down to the galley with her to watch *MacGyver* and let me prepare the carts. This meant I'd get to eat as many lobster medallions off the tops of the first-class salads as I wanted before she sent them up the elevator, and I really like lobster. It's an expensive habit for someone in my position, after I had to go on the run with zero notice. Don't get me wrong, I'd planned to disappear for a while. It's just that when the time came a few weeks ago, it did not go according to plan. At all. Far from it.

For example, I did not count on the kidnapping.

PART V

THE KIDNAPPING

Los Angeles Police Department
Los Angeles, CA
Incident Report # 9005127
Report Entered: March 10, 2013, 15:21:3, Officer John
Belvedere LAPD
Persons:
April Mae Manning
Role: Victim
Sex Age Race:
Female, 15, Caucasian
Officer Report: Responded to Cedars-Sinai Hospital pursuant to a call from staff regarding a complaint of kidnapping from a 14-year-old emergency admission. Upon arrival was directed to room 516 to find it empty. Recorded name and qualifying information of "victim" and directed staff to contact me if she resurfaced.

Preliminary Accident Report
WorldAir flight 1021, April 1, 2013
Present at transcript:
April May Manning, unaccompanied minor
Detective Jolette Henry, Albuquerque Police Department
Investigator Peter DeAngelo, NTSB
Statement:

April Manning:
Let me clarify something; I always *prepared* for getting kidnapped—all teenage girls should be, seeing as how we are such irresistible prey to rapist/killers, it's just a fact—but I didn't *count* on it as a rule. But still, you never know what can happen. They always say the odds are way against you for dying in a plane wreck, too, yet that's no comfort to me at all, for obvious reasons. In any event, it doesn't hurt to be safe. That's what they

teach you in the flight attendant manual. It's all about safety. And if you can't be safe, at least be resourceful.

So when the kidnapper came knocking on my door, I was prepared for two reasons. One, my mother and Grammy Mae are addicted to those true-crime shows on television, the ones that detail the terrible circumstances surrounding horribly murdered young people at the hands of sociopaths and serial killers. Almost always, their targets fall victim because they literally took one wrong step; like they stepped into the van with him (Ted Bundy), or they stepped inside his house (John Wayne Gacy, Jeffrey Dahmer), or they stepped aside to allow him into their own house (Derrick Todd Lee). One wrong step, remember? In instead of out. Forward instead of back.

My mother, who knew she was under court order to let me live half the time with someone who would mind me like a house plant, suddenly got all obsessed with teaching me how to fend for myself. She was the one who showed me all the YouTube videos on how to escape handcuffs, for example. She and Grammy Mae also took turns locking me in the trunks of both new and older-model car sedans, and then shouted the instructions at me on how to get my "own ass out." My mother knows I am big on lists, so she made lists for me all the time. Following is one of her lists that I kept folded up in my flight attendant manual. It's titled "Mom's Top Twenty Ways to Keep Your Young Ass from Gettin' Killed" (by the way, I realize this is a list-within-a-list, which is *awesome*) (and the word "ass," by the way, is not official profanity):

Mom's Top Twenty Ways to Keep Your Young Ass from Gettin' Killed

1. **Stay off the Internet.** I know that's impossible, but seriously, the Internet is just a giant bog of murdering, child-molesting masturbators. Seventy-seven percent of the

targets of Internet predators are fourteen and older. The first sign that you are vulnerable to Internet predators is thinking that you are not vulnerable to Internet predators.

2. **If a stranger approaches you** and tells you he's a famous photographer and you'd make a wonderful cover model, kick him in the gonads.

3. **Don't get married.** Sorry. When they say fifty-five percent of marriages end in divorce, they are not even counting the thousands of marriages that end in murder each year. Roughly a quarter of all female homicide victims got that way at the hands of a husband, boyfriend, or ex. Bad news, I know, but just bear that in mind.

4. **Lock the door.** Lord Christ. Derrick Todd Lee picked his victims just by jiggling doorknobs. Don't be an idiot.

5. **Don't go jogging down wooded paths all alone.** And if you do, don't make it worse by wearing earphones so you can't hear the killer coming up from behind. I swear, it's like the landscapers consulted rapists when they designed those paths.

6. **Learn how to escape from zip tie handcuffs.** It's easier than you think. Rapists and killers like to use zip ties to subdue their victims. (It doesn't hurt to learn how to escape from regular handcuffs, too. John Wayne Gacy tricked his victims into *putting the handcuffs on themselves*. Oh yeah—don't put the handcuffs on yourself!)

7. **Don't leave your door propped open.** For Christ's sake, that's how Ted Bundy killed two of his last three victims. Some bovine at a college sorority left the door propped open, and all Bundy had to do was step inside. And if you yourself are about to step into a secure building, for God's sake, don't hold the door open for the stranger behind you. Let them enter their passcode their own-ass self.

8. **Get a dog.** Preferably one with a big bark. Rapists really don't like dogs.

9. **Learn how to escape from a chokehold.** There are tons of tutorials on this on YouTube. (I know Number 1 on this list is to stay off the Internet, but I know you won't, so at least use its power for good.)

10. **If a stranger asks to use your phone, say no.** If a stranger is holding an unfolded map and asks you for directions, ignore him, or keep your distance and call out the information. If they ask you to get in the car and show them the way, don't you goddamn dare.

11. **If someone knocks on the door, don't open it.** Look through the window. If you don't recognize him, keep the door closed. If you do recognize him, like if he's an acquaintance or a neighbor, talk to him through the door. Twenty-seven percent of abducted kids are kidnapped by acquaintances. Pretend someone else is home. Call out something like, "Hey, Sluggo, someone's at the door!" And your dog should be barking, too.

12. **Never go near a man in a van.** Seriously.

13. **If a plainclothed stranger approaches you** anywhere in any situation (department store, gas station, side of the road, your own front door, etc.), shows you a badge, and/or tells you they are law enforcement and then says you have to leave with him, start screaming. Dial 911. Kick them. If it's a real police detective he should have known better. Tell him your mom said he deserved it.

14. **If you ever get lost in a crowded place,** pick *another mother* to ask for help. Less than ten percent of predators are female, so go with the odds.

15. **Never get in the car!** If someone pulls up beside you, points a gun at you, and demands that you get in the

car—don't! They probably won't call attention to themselves by shooting at you. And if they do, they only have a thirty percent chance of hitting you, and of that even a lower percent chance of hitting anything vital. Whereas if you get in the car, your pretty young ass is almost certainly dead—unless you jump out. Oh yeah, if you find yourself in the car, *jump out.*

16. **Learn how to escape from a locked car trunk.** Here are some tips: In recent-model cars, glow-in-the-dark escape handles have been installed for you to pull and free yourself. If you can't find an escape handle, yank out the wires to the taillights so the killer/rapist will get pulled over by the police.

17. **If someone jumps in your car,** pulls a weapon on you, and demands that you drive to a secluded area, jump out of the car and run. If you can't do that, then floor it and steer straight into the next streetlight. The airbag will deploy. You'll be fine—maybe a little banged up, but that's better than dead. If there is no streetlight nearby, rear-end a police car.

18. **Don't succumb to peer pressure!** Your friends are idiots. Don't listen to them when they say things like, "Drink this" (said the date rapist with the roofie cocktail), or, "It'll be fun" (said the soon-to-be-dead friend who wants to hitchhike to Bisbee), or, "It's not addictive if you only do it once" (said the crack dealer/future pimp).

19. **Improvise a weapon.** Plenty of everyday things can be deadly. Why do you think I wear a chopstick in my hair? If the day comes I won't think twice before shoving it into someone's jugular. Believe me.

20. **This bears repeating: Go for the gonads.** Don't be shy.

And two, the second reason I was prepared when I got abducted was because of *MacGyver*. Flo is also a mad *MacGyver* fan and now she and I are both red-star commentators on the *MacGyver* community website. That means we can post comments without having to wait for them to be screened by the moderators. You have to *earn* a status like that. Flo earned hers by pointing out that in episode fifteen of the first season, when Mac is making a homemade defibrillator, he uses a cable cut from a microphone as a power supply when—this is probably common knowledge to you—microphones don't have electricity running through them. So that was a huge faux pas on the part of the writers, and Flo is pretty legendary for pointing it out.

Flo has been flying for forty-six years. A funny thing about the airline business is that once someone gets hired they never quit, especially the flight attendants. The longer you have the job, the more control you have over the trips you can fly. So someone like my mother, with only seventeen years of seniority, is still relatively junior and would need a secret weapon to be awarded the "turnaround" trips with high flight hours that would still have her home in time to make me dinner. For example, a San Francisco turnaround, which would take her to SFO and back with no overnight layover to keep her away or connections to eat up her day, would put such a hefty chunk of hours on her schedule that just four of those trips each month was enough to maintain her full-time status.

This is the job the GAL said was bad for a single mother to have.

My mom worked as little as four days. A *month*. Thanks to the fact that she taught me the WorldAir crew computer interface. She needed to make sure none of her flights overlapped her custodial periods, because the common assumption about flight attendant mothers is that their jobs keep them from being able to care for their kids. It's a false assumption, and one that pilots never seem to face.

So I was her secret weapon. While my mom was working her trips and dealing with family court, I was working the flight attendant swap boards for her, grabbing those high-time trips when they showed up. I was good at it. My mother wasn't the only one I did it for. I processed bid schedules for my Grammy Mae (also a flight attendant), because her airline was an affiliate of WorldAir and their employee computer interface wasn't that different, and Flo Davenport, although both of them are so senior they hardly needed a secret weapon. By the way, the top five most popular trips to work, according to the WorldAir Atlanta-based flight attendant seniority graph, are (I love lists):

1. Narita
2. São Paulo
3. Buenos Aires
4. Honolulu
5. Beijing

These routes have high-time payouts and utilize the Boeing Triple Seven aircraft, which has the luxurious flight attendant rest area completely separate from the passenger cabin, where the crew can sleep fully reclined and watch movies if they want. Occasionally my mother got to fly those trips when I'd find one for her that fell during Ash's custodial time. I constantly worked the swap boards on her behalf, so that when a senior flight attendant needed to drop a prime-time trip, I was there to snatch it off the screen and move it to my mother's schedule before anyone else could get it. But never did my mother's job interfere with her custodial time with me—or her "court-ordered visitation," as Ash called it.

By the way, there is no such thing as court-ordered visitation (he also called it "court-supervised visitation"). It was just Ash's way of trying to make my mother sound crazy—to anyone who would listen—crazy as in an unfit mother. The fact was a lot less dramatic than that: my mother shared custody of me with her ex-husband Ash Manning, a man who is not my father, who adopted me when my mother really was in a vulnerable state after my dad's death. This gave Ash legal rights as though he were my real father. The shared custody schedule was bound by an "agreement" my mother was railroaded into signing under threat of the GAL's recommendation to the judge.

Ash Manning never had any use for me, so I didn't know why he was so hell-bent on that. As I got older I was determined to find out. Especially in light of recent events. Like the kidnapping.

When the knocking came of course I did not answer the door, seeing as how I'm good at minding my lists. And of course I had set the extra deadbolt. I'm a third-generation flight attendant (although a fake one for now). We always click the extra deadbolt.

At first when I heard the key in the lock I assumed Ash was home, so I had already begun grabbing my things to get ready to leave. But then I heard the knock and thought that was curious. Did Ash forget that the same key unlocked both the doorknob and the deadbolt? The knock came again. I tiptoed over.

I didn't look through the peephole on the door, because predators always expect you to look through that. I looked through a clear spot in the intricate stained-glass panel beside the door instead, because it gave a much better vantage. For example, I could see the person knocking was a no-neck stocky guy about five-foot-eleven with rheumy thyroid eyes behind glasses as thick as the bottom of glass bottles. He was wearing a blue jogging suit and a ridiculous pitch-black toupee. I could also see that his hands, which he hid behind his back, held two things: a large roll of silver electrical tape, and a packet of plastic zip-ties.

Then he said my name! "April," he called. "I'm Ash's friend. I'm a fellow pilot at WorldAir. I need to pick up some stuff for him. Can you let me in? He forgot to give me the key to the other lock."

I knew this guy was not a pilot for WorldAir. Pilots undergo mandatory retirement at the age of sixty, and this guy looked like he was a hundred years older than that. Also, his eyeglass lenses were thick as a stack of nickels. WorldAir didn't hire half-blind pilots. The kidnapping kit he held behind his back did not help his case, either. I turned to tiptoe away and got maybe four steps down the hall when he kicked the door open. He must have had feet like Frankenstein, because it took one single kick and that was it. *Bang!* It was way louder than I expected.

I thought I'd have more time to make it to the sliding glass doors and out the side patio, but no. He moved fast for a big fossil, and my backpack didn't help me, either. He grabbed it like it was a convenient handle and pulled me back. I ineffectively kicked and scratched. Suddenly it occurred to me to be terrified, and the fear gripped me like a giant squid. I began to scream.

"Shut up, you lousy little brat!" he growled at me.

I did not shut up. I screamed so loud my face felt on fire. I was surprised no one came to my rescue. I think if I were screaming like this in Atlanta someone would have at least meandered over out of curiosity. I managed to wriggle free from the backpack, but then he caught me by the arm, grabbed my hair, and dragged me back to the foyer with his hand over my mouth. I could smell the nicotine on his fingers, and he didn't even seem to flinch when I bit his leathery hand so hard I was surprised I didn't draw blood.

I'd like to take a second here to clarify something. Even after all my supposed preparation, it's a lot harder than you think to fight off a man who's built like a big cinderblock with hands like anvils. I even kicked him square in the crotch, and it didn't seem to break his stride. He flipped me on my stomach like a rodeo calf, and tried to zip-tie my hands. My extreme objection to this was making itself evident. I wasn't nicknamed after the Tasmanian Devil for nothing. I was even beginning to think I was wearing him down, when suddenly I felt a wet cloth over my nose and mouth. It smelled exactly like nail-polish remover, only ten times the potency.

I wondered how Old Cinderblock got nail-polish remover, because he didn't have it when he kicked down the door. Then I felt an immediate weakness take over my body, reducing my fighting to a few anemic kicks and twists. Thick fuzz quickly closed in on the periphery of my vision, and amid the sound of Old Cinderblock calling me every profanity in the book—the real profanities, not the ones Officer Ned uses—I heard another voice, deep and drawn out, like it was carried across caverns on the echoes of the wind.

"The same key fit both locks, you idiot," Kathy said, and then I blacked out.

CHAPTER 4

I awoke when my head bumped against the back fender of Cinderblock's car. Whatever he used to knock me out didn't have much of a lasting effect, but I kept myself limp like a sack of birdseed so he'd think I was still unconscious. My hands and ankles were bound together by zip ties, and it felt like he'd wrapped that silver electrical tape over my mouth and around the back of my head at least three times.

He was not *at all* gentle flipping me around while unlocking his trunk. And I seriously cannot even believe no one intervened or called 911 or anything. Granted, Ash's driveway was secluded by high hedges, but still, in Atlanta we would have had at least four people filming this on their cell phones by now.

Old Cinderblock plunked me in his trunk, threw my backpack in on top of me, and slammed the hood down. He was cussing up a flood of filth, too. I heard him and Kathy take their places in the front seats, and soon I felt the car backing out of Ash's driveway. I thought it would be best to lie still for a few minutes until I was certain the car was in a populated area. It was early March, so dusk was setting in early as well. The trunk was not airtight, but it was light tight, and I could not see a thing.

I especially could not see any glow-in-the-dark escape handle. These kinds of emergency trunk releases have been required on all non-hatchback vehicles since the 2002 model year. So this was either a sedan built before then—which would not have surprised me, because the trunk alone was practically bigger than the laundry room Ash expected me to sleep in—or the handle had been removed, which raised the hair on my arms. Why would you remove the emergency-release handle from inside a trunk unless you were planning to trap people inside?

First I had to get out of the zip ties. They were the standard kind you buy at the hardware store. Luckily he'd bound my hands in front of me instead of behind my back. Zip ties, contrary to popular thought, are not that strong. But like those Chinese finger traps, they can seem deceptively impenetrable if you struggle with them in the wrong way.

I knew more than one method to get out of zip ties, but in this instance I simply used the quickest way I knew how. Here's a rundown for the ones around my wrists:

1. With my teeth, I gripped the excess tab extending from the locking toggle to tighten the zip tie around my wrists as much as possible.
2. I extended my elbows on either side of me as far as they would go, creating maximum tension on the super-tight zip tie.
3. I raised my arms (still bound at the wrists) above my head as high as I could (luckily it was pretty high because the trunk was spacious), then yanked them down toward my torso with a mighty snap while simultaneously yanking my elbows apart. ("Remember to yank your arms down *and* out at the same time," my mother and Grammy Mae had taught me. "Down *and* out.")

The zip tie popped off my wrists like a party favor. The trick is in the tension, I was told. To deal with the one around my ankles, I grasped the toes of my feet and yanked them toward me as hard as I could while pulling my knees apart. Off it popped. In the darkness I heard a small piece of glass shatter as my knee banged against something dense. I ignored the tape around my mouth for the moment, snatched up my backpack, and felt for the blue aluminum carabiner I kept clipped inside. A carabiner is a metal loop with a spring-loaded gate commonly used as a keychain, and this one was useful because it came equipped with a tiny LED flashlight built in along its length. It provided all the light of an anemic firefly, but still it was a godsend right then.

The car lurched along slowly so I figured we were stuck in the famous L.A. traffic. We hadn't driven far enough to have made it to the freeway yet, so I thought that was encouraging. I could hear Old Cinderblock griping to Kathy, who ignored him and must have been texting, because I could hear the continuous telltale cell phone pings.

"Doll, I thought you said this was gonna be easy," Cinderblock groused. "I've had cartel bodyguards go down easier than that little wildcat. And you neglected to tell me this was a double package."

"Don't call me doll," she finally responded, her voice as empty as an air pocket, "and it's not my fault I had to improvise. It needed to look like she never made it home."

A familiar fury boiled in my chest. I didn't think my opinion of that woman could have gotten any lower, but now here a trap door opened to reveal an entire Grand Canyon of awfulness about her. Even my overactive imagination had not begun to graze the tip of the monstrous gutter rat she really was.

While we were stopped I could hear the bustling of curbside parking and retail activity, so I figured we were still on Manhattan Beach Boulevard. Then the car lurched forward, signaling a green light, which kicked me back into gear. I did a quick scan with the pin light along the hatch seal looking for a release handle again in case I just missed it the first time, but to no avail. So I immediately began pulling out the taillight housing and yanking the wires. With that done, I focused on one taillight and tried to knock out its bulb and casing to create an opening big enough to stick my hand through. It's been proven in the past that a frantically waving hand where a taillight should be is a good way to catch the attention of other motorists.

But this must have been an early model car, because the taillight portal was too small to be punched through with my fist. So I twisted around and shone the pin light toward the back of the trunk. Maybe there was a jack kit with a crowbar in it. I was encouraged to see the big bundle covered in a coarse army blanket that my knee had hit earlier. Great, I thought, *stuff*! There was bound to be something useful in there. I whipped away the blanket, shone the dim light on its contents, and began screaming.

CHAPTER 5

Gaping at me, her large eyes vacuous and dead, her ice-blond hair spiked with blood, was my friend Jalyce.

My screams were muffled by the electrical tape still wrapped around my mouth and head, so thankfully Cinderblock and Kathy didn't hear me over the car radio. Tears welled in my eyes and ran down my cheeks, loosening the adhesive on the tape, which I pulled down below my mouth so I could breathe better. Poor Jalyce; she had given me a ride home from the arrival gate that afternoon.

You neglected to tell me this was a double package.

I had to improvise. It needed to look like she never made it home.

My crying began to turn into ragged gasps. If not for me, Jalyce would still be alive. Her child would still have a mother. I had to clasp my hand over my mouth, because low-pitched keening sounds were escaping from my throat. I closed my eyes tightly, and I was a nanosecond from detonating into full-on freak mode when suddenly I heard my mother's voice descend on my mind like a calming breath: "Don't freak out, girl. *Figure* it out."

I stifled my sobs and forced myself to focus. Jalyce was gone, that was certain. She had already started to stiffen. "I'm sorry," I whispered. It was a statement weighted with such truth I almost felt she heard me. I took her eyeglasses from her jacket pocket—my knee had earlier shattered one of the lenses—and put them in my backpack. Her employee badge was still clipped to a lanyard around her neck, and I took that, too, as well as a small pocketbook at her side. The trunk was lined with a plastic tarp, but I dug through that, found the flap in the trunk's carpet lining indicating the jack compartment, then pulled out the kit, careful to be quiet.

No crowbar was inside, just a standard scissor jack minus the detachable handle to operate it. But I didn't grow up the granddaughter of an aircraft engineer (not to mention the grandniece of an airline mechanic) without picking up a few things. So I twisted the end bolt by hand until the jack expanded to the point it was tightly pressed against the floor and roof of the trunk.

"The interstate is ahead," I heard Kathy tell Cinderblock. "Get in the left lane and take 405 south."

My fingers alone weren't strong enough to turn the bolt and raise the jack further; I needed more leverage. From my backpack I grabbed one of my mother's sturdy lacquered chopsticks and inserted it through the jack bolt to create a crank handle. From there I kept cranking the jack against the roof until the pressure proved stronger than the lock and —thank you, Lord Jesus God Christ on the Cross, as Flo would say—it popped open.

Quickly I reached out to capture the trunk lid so it wouldn't fly up and draw the attention of the detestable duo up front, and, just as the left-turn light changed to green, I slid quietly from the trunk to the asphalt below and pressed the lid back down, grateful that, though wonky, it still clicked shut. I skirmished toward the startled drivers of the three cars behind me. None of them unlocked their doors to allow me inside, even though I patted pleadingly on their passenger-side windows. None of them even immediately flipped open their phones to dial 911 that I could see. (And you wonder why I have trust issues.) Instead, they simply followed Old Cinderblock onto the interstate, leaving me behind to be grateful my escape had gone unnoticed by the bickering pricks in the old Chevy Impala with my friend's corpse in the trunk.

I stood at the intersection of Manhattan Beach Boulevard and Inglewood Avenue. In this part of L.A. the neighborhoods go from good to bad to gang-banger in a matter of blocks, and I was definitely no longer in the nice parts. I could see jet planes landing in the near distance, which gave me comfort because it meant LAX was nearby, and airports comforted me. I ducked into a dilapidated Circle K convenience store and stumbled toward the lady behind the counter, who was engrossed in something on her laptop. I begged her to call 911, which, surprisingly, she did without question.

"We gotta girl here who look like she been tied up and dragged behind a truck," the lady said into the receiver. "Uh oh, now she cryin'. You better hurry, this po' child in *distress.*"

We were the only people inside, so I sank to the floor with my back against the counter. I saw my reflection in the aluminum of the reach-in cooler opposite me, and gasped. The twisted electrical tape stuck to my tufted hair and still circled my throat like a terrible necklace. My right eyelid drooped heavily because a large hematoma had formed at the bruise on my forehead where Old Cinderblock had banged it against his fender before tossing me in the trunk. My wrists and ankles still bore red marks from the zip ties. My white T-shirt was torn, filthy, and, curiously, covered in blood. No wonder no one had let me in their car, I thought.

But the blood . . . what was with the blood? I wasn't bleeding, was I? Then it hit me like a bag of nickels: it wasn't *my* blood. It was Jalyce's blood.

The convenience-store lady clucked at me reassuringly and offered me some Gatorade, which I accepted gratefully. She was a sizeable African American woman and her name tag identified her as LaVonda Morgenstern. She wore her hair cropped very close to her scalp, and large earrings carved from coconut shells hung to her shoulders. I could see the botched removal of a gang symbol tattoo on her arm, and around her wrist was a thick bracelet made of embroidery thread that bore the rainbow colors of the gay community.

I flinched when the bell on the door rang, indicating a customer had opened it. "Out!" LaVonda called at him. "Go on! Get out! Can't you see we in *distress* here?"

The startled customer backed up and closed the door softly, and LaVonda locked it after him and flipped the Closed sign. She busied herself gathering things for my aid, talking all the while. "You don't have to tell me what happened, child, but I can tell it ain't have been good. All I'm gonna say is if some nasty bastard got to you in a bad way, you can't be washing nothing off. I know it's hard, 'cause the first thing you wanna do is jump into a barrel of battery acid to get it off you, but that shit be evidence, 'scuse my language . . . ."

She continued on and on, covering my shoulders with her large insulated windbreaker, making a compress by wrapping a bag of ice in a souvenir I Heart L.A. T-shirt and instructing me to hold it to my head, then changing the subject to more pleasant matters, like how her wife was pregnant with their second baby, and they were gonna name the child Dixie LaRue if it was a girl, and Jacques if it was a boy, only she pronounced the name "Ja-QUEZ."

It occurred to me the Gatorade, the jacket, the steady stream of talking was LaVonda's way of keeping me from slipping into shock. I didn't think she needed to worry, but then that's what all people about to go into shock think. It wasn't until I stopped shivering violently that I realized I'd been shivering at all. Wow, they teach you about this stuff in the first aid section of the WorldAir flight attendant manual, but when it really happens it still seems to come out of nowhere.

The ambulance arrived before the police. LaVonda told them the little she knew, told me to go with them and that she'd inform the police where I went when they got there. She squeezed my hand and said, simply, "Be strong now, girl." As we backed out of the parking lot, I marveled at how the good—and bad—in people can show itself at the most unexpected times.

The ambulance took me to Cedars-Sinai Hospital, where the ER nurses patched me up and put me in a fifth-floor room with a shower so I could clean myself up, which I did gratefully. I smoothed my wet hair with the comb from the amenity kit they gave me, and lay on the hospital bed waiting for the police to come, which seemed to be taking forever. My bloody clothes and shoes had been left in the emergency area and replaced with a hospital gown. I padded barefoot to the door and was surprised to find it locked from the outside. I knocked loudly and began to call out. "Hey, why am I locked in here?"

A stern voice answered me through the door. "Stay put, young lady. We're just following the protocol for runaways. Your guardian's on the way to pick you up."

"What guardian? I don't have a guardian! Let me out of here. I need to talk to the police!" I shrieked. I dashed to the bedside phone and tried to dial 911, but the cradle had no dial. The phone was for incoming calls only. I frantically pushed the nurse buzzer, only to be yelled at by the guard at the door to stop. Then—and I had to shake my head to make sure I wasn't imagining it—I heard Kathy's voice call out to him from down the hall.

"Pardon me, but is it really necessary to shout at her like that?"

"Who are you?"

"I'm April Manning's guardian ad litem. Here's the judge's order. My name is Catherine Galleon."

"Great, come with me to the nurses station to sign the release papers."

What? Kathy wasn't my guardian ad litem! Was she?

I stood frozen, not in shock or fear, but suspended in that flash of a moment before instincts take over, when you "assess your conditions" like they teach you in flight attendant training. My conditions, though, appeared pretty dismal.

The bathroom had no window, and even if it did I was too high up for a window to be any good. And regarding resources, there was just the hospital bed with an empty meal tray perched on it. What was I supposed to . . . then suddenly I jumped into action.

I grabbed the meal tray, broke off its flimsy metal legs, and tied them together like a bundle of sticks using the ties I ripped off the back of my hospital gown.

Then I slid the long end of the flat tray—which was made of melamine, thin but very strong—under the hinge-side of the door just far enough to be flush with the edge on the other side. I lifted the other end of the tray and rolled the bundle of bound metal beneath it, creating a sort of seesaw. From there I stepped firmly down on the elevated end of the tray, and the ensuing leverage hoisted the door a half an inch, which was plenty to lift it off its hinges so I could prop the door ajar enough for me to sneak through. I was careful to ensure it remained erect and did not noisily slam down on the linoleum floor—then I grabbed my backpack and slipped into the hall and then into the stairwell without looking back to see if anyone had noticed. Thank you, season one, episode six of *MacGyver.*

I ran down one flight of stairs before I remembered I was naked but for a hospital gown with no ties. So I stopped and rifled through my backpack to find the damp souvenir T-shirt LaVonda had used to wrap my ice compress. I put that on, tied my hospital gown around my waist like a towel and peeked into the hallway of the floor below mine. I saw nothing useful, so I descended to the next floor and then the next, until I saw what looked to be an open linen closet. I snuck inside and grabbed a pair of blue hospital scrubs and put them on, including the mask and cap and the elasticized booties over my feet.

And this is how I departed through the side door of the Cedars-Sinai emergency room, just as a cluster of security officers were rushing inside to answer the alert call regarding an escaped delinquent.

A bus was parked at the stop across the street, so I jumped on it not caring where it was headed. I showed my transit card to the driver and was relieved to hear the bus was headed to a stop near the airport. I disembarked across the street from Hertz Rent-a-Car, then caught their shuttle to the WorldAir departure area, where I presented my mother's badge at the employee line through security.

The fact that I was in hospital scrubs alarmed nobody. Almost all flight attendants have second jobs. I know of at least two who are nurses, several who are attorneys, and one who is the mayor of a small town in Tennessee. I planned to tell the security guard I was out of uniform because I was off the clock but needed to complete some computer-based training in the employee lounge.

But all she asked me was "How'd you get that shiner?"

"Unruly crack-addict gunshot victim," I answered.

She waved me through and I gathered my things off the x-ray conveyor, hurried to the WorldAir concourse, and went down the stairs to the large, windowless cluster of hallways and communal rest areas deep in the bowels of the LAX airport that houses the crew lounge. I stayed there for two and a half days. My constant presence went undetected because everyone else was in transit. It's why the WorldAir crew lounges are the perfect places to hide.

First task at hand was to assess my resources. I withdrew Jalyce's small pocketbook from my backpack and opened it to discover that it was not her pocketbook at all, but Kathy's. *Awesome*, I thought. I looked at the name on her driver's license and saw that, indeed, the horrid little ferret's full name was actually Catherine Galleon Landry.

Kathy's small wallet contained one hundred and sixty dollars in cash, which I gratefully folded and tucked into the side pocket of my backpack along with her driver's license, a slip of paper covered in some nearly indecipherable scribbling and penciled notations (all I could make out were the words "angel" and "angels," which I found hugely ironic), and a small plastic device the size of a playing card with a clip on the back that at first I took to be Ash's garage-door opener.

Funny, I thought, *why didn't she give this to Cinderblock instead of the key?* It would have given him carte blanche access to the condo, because the door leading to the garage from the kitchen didn't even have a lock.

But upon closer inspection I saw the device wasn't a garage-door opener at all—or at least not Ash's. Instead of a clicker, it had a small screen on the front for a digital display. So whatever it was, it was going in my backpack with the other pertinent items I recovered from her purse.

Everything else—the purse, the small wallet, a few credit cards, a tube of lipstick, and a packet of condoms (yuck)—I divided among all the trash receptacles throughout the facility. Other than the driver's license, it didn't look like Kathy had lost much to slow her down. The small purse was probably just an auxiliary bag, because I'd seen her usual purse and it was big enough to easily fit a bunch of severed heads inside.

Over the next few days, I grabbed what I could from the lost-and-found room—a small Rollaboard, a pair of purple flip flops, a pair of men's comfortably worn size 7 regulation loafers, some uniform pieces that could also pass for regular clothes—and stealthily committed petty thievery from the bags of dozing flight attendants to get the rest. A word of advice: those supposedly TSA-approved, candy-colored luggage locks? They're a piece of cake to pick. Ash used them regularly, which cracked me up. (To the girl who reached her layover to discover all her makeup and underwear had disappeared from her bag, I say sorry and thank you.)

The second day, once I was presentable, I asked the guy at the supervisor window to please check on "our colleague" Jalyce Sanders. I told him I heard she'd been hurt or something, and I wanted to know where to send the flowers. He pulled up Jalyce's schedule and said, "Well, she must have recovered, because her schedule is normal. I don't see any absences."

"Wait . . . what?"

"Yeah, she came in today a few hours ago. She's working the gate to Atlanta this afternoon."

I thanked him and walked away, rubbing my temples. I knew that was Jalyce I had seen in the trunk of Old Cinderblock's Impala. I still had her broken tortoiseshell eyeglasses and her employee badge in my bag. I knew she was dead. I knew it. I thought about calling the police again, but look what happened last time. I'm an *unaccompanied minor*. Evidently all Kathy had to do was show up with a court order and, *boom!*, suddenly I'm the one who gets locked up and treated like a criminal.

I was sure the police would simply follow protocol, hand me over, and assume it would be sorted out later. Remember Jeffrey Dahmer? The Milwaukee serial killer who cooked his victims like a stew and kept their body parts hanging around like a human BBQ smokehouse? One of his victims—a naked and bleeding fourteen-year-old—actually escaped and called 911, only to have the police officers *hand the kid back to Dahmer*, who'd told them he was responsible for the boy, and they believed him simply because he was older and it was easier that way.

It was sorted out later, of course, when police were sifting through the decaying pile of corpses at Dahmer's place and—"Oh, looky, there's the severed head of that kid from earlier." [Palm slap to the head.] "Make sure to notate that."

So no, I have no illusions about how my rights as a minor would play out at the precinct with Kathy standing there waving a paper signed by a judge. They'd hand me over like a bouquet of roses. Are you kidding? I'm an unaccompanied minor. I have no rights.

And Ash—who knew where he fit into all this? At first I assumed he was the one who put Kathy up to all this, but then why bother with Old Cinderblock if that were the case?

Plus, Ash had e-mailed me twice since I'd been abducted. They were the same vitriol he usually expected me to pass on to my mother, this time about how he was going to drag her back into court because it was her fault that the wallpaper on my iPad depicted a bunch of naked men.

It didn't. My iPad wallpaper depicted a collection of artwork by Michelangelo, such as the statue of David and the paintings on the ceiling of the Sistine Chapel, which, in the real world, would be considered masterpieces of the Renaissance. But, again, family court doesn't exist in the real world.

Anyway, Ash's e-mails showed no sign that he knew or cared whether I was missing. It seemed to me that if Ash wanted to track me down so his cronies could finish a botched hit, he would have tried to trick me into revealing where I was. I'd known him since I was four, so I was pretty versed in his duplicity. If he was trying to put one over on me, it would have read as inauthentic as a big bag of breast implants. So I was reservedly skeptical about his involvement in all this, but still considered him a vain, worm-hearted weasel.

The next day I felt prepared to leave the lounge. The bruise on my forehead had diminished to where it could be hidden by makeup, I had an adequate supply of clothes and amenities, plus I was beginning to have repeated run-ins with the same people as they passed through the lounge on their way to work their trips. So I used the company computer to access my mother's employee interface, booked myself jumpseat on a flight to Detroit, printed out my boarding voucher, and ventured upstairs.

I looked around the concourse to be assured no one would come running to tackle me, and was relieved to encounter the customary crowd of self-focused bovines as far as the eye could see, so I slipped into it seamlessly. On the way to the Detroit flight, I passed the Atlanta gate and stopped at a distance to see what I could make of it. I didn't recognize the person there, so I came closer until I was standing directly across the counter from the gate agent.

"Can I help you?" She smiled at me expectantly. Her badge read Jalyce Sanders; her face read anything but.

"No," I said. "I just thought you were somebody I knew."

CHAPTER 6

Since then I've kept the events of that day at Ash's condo to myself, except I sent an anonymous e-mail to Officer Ned imploring him to please look into the disappearance—and stolen identity—of Jalyce Sanders. I tried to be as detailed as possible without revealing my identity, including the involvement of Kathy Landry and describing Old Cinderblock, his car, and most of his car's license plate numbers—but I had no idea if he did as I asked. I sincerely hoped so. Aside from Officer Ned, I don't trust the police, for obvious reasons, and I didn't want to endanger my mother and other family members—including Flo—by putting them on my radar as I'd done to poor Jalyce. Again, I'd spent the last few weeks in a literal holding pattern, trying to determine my next move. I no longer communicated with my mother via Skype, but rather through e-mail. As long as she knew I was okay, she didn't push for details. She assumed I was at Ash's place, and I didn't correct her.

And my grandparents? Ash had issued a protective order barring them from coming into physical contact with me. It had to do with "not allowing" me to celebrate Easter, a move that was surprisingly effective in the Bible Belt. I kept in contact with them via e-mail as well. I didn't have to worry about running into Grammy Mae because she worked a regional airline and rarely traveled nonrevenue, and Poppa Max hated to nonrev. He was so content with his vegetable garden that it kind of warmed your heart. I wish things were that simple for me.

My father's parents were gone. My grandfather Roy, the airline engineer who used to let me help him study for his annual recurrent training, died a year and a half ago when the jack supporting the vintage Ford Rambler he was restoring collapsed and crushed his chest. That was a bad day. I was nuts about him. We used to spend every Sunday afternoon conducting experiments and testing the viability of any number of inventions he'd concocted over the years. He had a large barn at the back of his property, and it was packed with gadgets and motorized pulleys and levers. It was like Willy Wonka's chocolate factory in there, only with machines. Talk about a personal paradise. When we got the news, I remember my mother sitting on the couch and crying almost as hard as she did when my dad died.

"He was such a good man," she sobbed. I sat on the floor crying as well, and rested my head against her knee, patting her calves until we both seemed to feel better.

My father's mother had passed away when he was a boy, from hypobaropathy (or altitude sickness) while climbing Mount Kilimanjaro with a group of fellow flight attendants on a ten-day layover in Tanzania during the late seventies. She and Flo had been best friends, having graduated from the same flight attendant training class in 1967.

I kept a picture of them in my backpack. In it, she and Flo are standing in the massive engine well of a WorldAir jet, each wearing one of those iconic pink-and-orange uniforms designed by Pucci for WorldAir stewardesses back in the day. The uniform consisted of a short tunic over nearly-as-short hot pants, and white patent-leather boots. Their bleached platinum-blond hair is styled in the volumized cascade that was popular then, with a center strand clipped at the crown like Nancy Sinatra on the cover of her *These Boots Were Made for Walkin'* single. Their youth and beauty are absolutely incandescent.

When I looked at their picture, I'd get flooded with a nostalgia I'm not nearly old enough to feel. Wow, I think, it must have been so *insanely amazing* to be a stewardess back then, and my heart swells with pride. I kept the picture pressed in a compact flipbook along with those of the rest of my family. One each. I had to keep it light. None of my family members had any idea I lived in the air. Only Flo knew that secret, and never pressed me on why it needed to be kept.

PART VI

THE BOMB THREATS

Preliminary Accident Report, cont.
WorldAir flight 1021, April 1, 2013
Present at transcript:
April May Manning, unaccompanied minor
Detective Jolette Henry, Albuquerque Police Department
Investigator Peter DeAngelo, NTSB
Investigator Anthony Kowalski, FBI

Investigator Peter DeAngelo, NTSB:
April, Agent Kowalski of the FBI has arrived and he has some questions for you as well.
April Manning:
I spoke to him on the phone!
DeAngelo:
Exactly. Here he is now. I'm leaving for a bit to get a cup of coffee and let him take over for a while. Can I get you anything?
April Manning:
Yes, please. A Gatorade and a blanket, please.
DeAngelo:
Fine. Agent Kowalski, maybe you can help her get around to describing how she committed the federal crime of breaching the cockpit of an operational aircraft.
Investigator Anthony Kowalski, FBI:
April Manning, I take it?
April Manning:
Nice to meet you—
Kowalski:
Yeah, right. Listen, the first thing I want to know from you, young lady, is this: How the hell did you manage to throw a dead man off an aircraft *during flight*?
April Manning:
I should start with the bomb threats.
Kowalski:

That would be good.

April Manning:

When Ash first won custody of me, it was Malcolm's suggestion that I write a letter to Judge Cheevers threatening to bomb a plane.

"Since your stepdad is now your primary physical custodian," he said, "he is responsible for everything you do now. Before, when your mother had custody, you never threatened to bomb things, right?"

"Right."

"So this would be a new development in your behavior. It would constitute a 'change in circumstance,' so when you go back to court and get a real guardian ad litem this time, as opposed to some sucking bottom fish, you can reverse everything."

"Genius," I told him.

"Thank you," he said.

Another genius thing about Malcolm is that he finagled Captain Beefheart, real-live "emotional support" dog, out of his parents during the divorce. It was his guardian ad litem's suggestion, and the only thing she did for him that seemed to put his welfare at a precedent. Now Malcolm has official papers and can bring Beefheart on board every flight, and he doesn't even have to keep him in his carrier. Not once has Beefheart ever pooped on the plane, that I know of. There was that unfortunate time when he peed in the aisle, though.

Malcolm acted like this was just pulling the wool over his parents' eyes, but I could see how the dog really helped him with the perpetual transition from coast to coast. Beefheart was the most constant thing in Malcolm's life. He was pretty constant in my life, too, come to think of it.

And Captain Beefheart is not some pedigree puffball, like you'd expect from someone as rich as Malcolm. Instead, the dog is a Dumpster mutt with a half-chewed-off ear that looks like a baby crocodile covered in fur. In reality, Beefheart is a corgi/pit bull muttigree mix. He was found by a trash man who heard a puppy yelping inside the truck compactor. He dug it out and dropped it off at a rescue organization in Georgia called Angels Among Us.

Beefheart was then trained in an experimental program instigated by the Fulton County Penitentiary that used prison inmates to train the animals, which included all kinds of creatures like spider monkeys and even miniature horses. Malcolm qualified for a support animal about six months ago, owing to the amount of time he'd flown as an unaccompanied minor.

"All I had to do was tell the court-ordered co-parenting counselor I cried a lot on the airplane (Malcolm never cried that I saw), and *boom!*, instant prescription for Captain Beefheart."

The prisoners get to name the pets they trained, and Captain Beefheart came already christened. Malcolm learned it was in honor of an avant-garde musician who'd gained cult fame during the seventies and early eighties.

"Still, why Captain Beefheart of all things?" I wondered.

"Maybe Frank Zappa was too mainstream," Malcolm responded.

Beefheart had an official green vest, and was cleared by World-Air to board all aircraft. Much of Beefheart's extensive training was unnecessary for Malcolm's purposes. For example, Malcolm didn't need Beefheart to flip light switches and only had him retrieve things for him for fun.

"How cool is *this*?" Malcolm would exclaim, dispatching Beefheart up the aisle to nip some extra pretzel packets off the back of the snack cart.

"Can you send him back for some cookies, too?" I'd ask, impressed.

"Of course." And off Beefheart would go to the quiet cheers of the nearby passengers.

I loved that dog. He made me wish I had one of my own to bring on the plane. I remember my mother tried to assign me one, but because Ash was my primary physical custodian and held sway with decision-making authority on all aspects of my life, of course he vetoed anything that would make it easier for me to deal with my present circumstances.

So I'd use my mother's password to pull up a preliminary flight summary to see if an emotional support animal was listed on the departure report. Nine times out of ten, on the flights to LAX out of ATL and vice versa, it was Captain Beefheart. It was a reliable way of discerning the pattern of Malcolm's flight habits. Luckily they often coincided with Flo's flight habits, especially since Flo let me put in the bids for her trips every month. So, even though I should have been used to it, my heart still skipped a beat when I saw him. Even on this fateful flight, up until the hijacking, I was so happy to see Malcolm on the plane.

FBI subject log, April 1, 2013, 13:34:

1. April Mae Manning
- Born: April 1, 1998 (15 years old today)
- Caucasian female, light brown shoulder-length hair, green eyes, 5'6", 105 lbs.
- Identifying marks: Large scar, right arm

- Parents:
- Elizabeth Davenport Manning (divorced)
- Flight Attendant, WorldAir
- Born: November 16, 1974 (39 years old)

- Robert Madison Coleman (deceased October 12, 2003)
- Flight Attendant, WorldAir
- Born: September 16, 1974 (29 at time of death)

- Ash Underwood Manning (divorced)
- Pilot, WorldAir
- Born: March 15, 1967 (49 years old)
- Adoptive father, primary physical custodian

2. Malcolm Jeffrey Colgate (14 years old)
- Born: January 2, 1998
- Caucasian male, red wavy hair, brown eyes, 5'5", 95 lbs.
- Identifying marks: Freckles

- Parents:
- Matilda Marie Remington Colgate (divorced)
- Morton McGill Colgate (divorced)
- Founders, Global Colgate Enterprises, under investigation for tax fraud since April 2010.

3. Edward Thornton Rockwell (42 years old) (single)
- Born: August 11, 1970
- African American male, brown hair, brown eyes, 6'5", 195 lbs.
- Identifying marks: Scar, left shoulder, bullet entry wound. Scar, upper left torso, bullet entry wound. Scar, upper left back, bullet exit wound.
- Law Enforcement Officer, Atlanta Fulton County Police Department
- Date of employment: January 16, 1993
- Record of employment: 12 disciplinary actions. Discharge of firearm resulting in death of suspect. 14 interdepartmental accolades. Request for advancement: Declined 1998, 2002, 2007, 2012.

4. Florence "Flo" Beulah Butterfield Schnieder Chang Davenport (67 years old) (divorced)

- Caucasian female, white hair, blue eyes, 5'0", 95 lbs.
- Identifying marks: Birthmark, right hip. Tattoo ("Mac-Gyver"), right ankle. Pierced belly button.
- Flight Attendant, WorldAir
- Born: February 15, 1946
- Date of employment: March 20, 1967
- Record of employment: 7 incidents of "failure to appear," 5 suspended terminations, 14 disciplinary marks for behavior described as "wantonly insubordinate," 1,423 passenger appreciation letters.

5. Captain Beefheart (approx. 2 years old)
- Emotional Support Animal
- Mixed-breed corgi/pit bull male canine. Rescued from Dumpster by Angels Among Us Pet Rescue. Trained by the Atlanta inmate program. Certified January 15, 2013.
- Identifying marks: Prominent teeth. Mild halitosis. Partial missing left ear.

Kowalski:

Here's your Gatorade and blanket.

April Manning:

Thanks.

Kowalski:

Now get back to explaining how events transpired today.

April Manning:

I noticed the first sign that something was wrong with World-Air flight 1021 during boarding of the aircraft, after Malcolm and I had taken our seats and were engaged in our usual pre-flight banter.

"PSA flight 182," Malcolm challenged.

"Puh-leez." I rolled my eyes, trying to suppress my elation over seeing him. "PSA flight 182 crashed over San Diego in 1978 when it collided with a two-seater Cessna. Everyone on board both aircrafts died, plus seven people on the ground."

"The pilot of the Cessna had a heart attack and lost control of his equipment," Malcolm added as he situated Captain Beefheart in his soft-sided crate under the seat in front of him.

"A common misconception," I chided. "Actually, the NTSB concluded it was the PSA pilot's error when he failed to follow the tower's instructions to maintain a visual of the private plane."

"Really?" Malcolm answered. "Well, what were the pilot's last words on the black-box recording?"

"I don't know," I lied. Okay, sometimes I do throw him a few softballs.

"He said, 'We're going down. Tell my mother I love her.'" Actually, the doomed pilot had said, "Ma, I love ya," but I didn't want to be a stickler.

"Wow, good one." I widened my eyes like Flo told me to. Flo was pretty good at flirting with men. She'd divorced four husbands, who all remained devoted to her. "The best husband is an ex-husband," she liked to tell me. I didn't exactly agree with everything she said, though, as I don't understand the reason people get married in the first place.

Malcolm and I were in row 44 next to the window on the pilot's side of the aircraft. This was the D section of the plane, which is the area all the way back by the lavatories. I swore I could still smell the cigarettes people used to smoke back there before they banned smoking on domestic flights in the early nineties. Malcolm gathered Captain Beefheart from his crate and handed him to me.

"There won't be any private planes in our path today," he said, "because the legacy of that crash set a precedent for tower-to-pilot protocol. A crash like that can never happen again."

"I know that," I guffawed. I kissed Captain Beefheart on his eyelids. He had the kind of eyes that look like they are rimmed in eyeliner, incongruously feminine against the rest of his crocodile exterior. "What about Swissair flight 111?"

"An MD-11 en route to Geneva, Switzerland. It crashed off the coast of Halifax, Nova Scotia, in 1998. An electrical fire on board grew out of control."

"And . . . ."

"And what?" he asked.

"And if the pilot hadn't tried to circle to dump fuel before landing, they would have made it safely to the emergency landing."

"I wouldn't call it 'safely,'" he countered.

"Still, you know, that last attempt to circle cost them the vessel," I went on, my success at flirting losing air like a punctured life raft.

"We see things differently," Malcolm said, nudging me. It was an inside joke, and it made me smile. He knew I was right, though. The electrical fire of Swissair flight 111 was not the pilot's fault, but the decision to circle was. But who can blame the pilot? That is what the rules required of him—dump the fuel before an emergency landing. Pilots are rule followers. But flight attendants are different. Even in my flight attendant manual, it says expressly that when the rules don't apply . . . you are free to improvise.

It was because of my lively discussion with Malcolm about plane wrecks that the flight attendant approached us before take-off. Another passenger had complained to him about our conversation, so he made his way to our row to admonish us.

"Zip it, kids," he said curtly. "Nobody wants to hear a play-by-play of past plane wrecks. And what's with the dog?"

"He's an emotional support animal," Malcolm said. "He's registered on the manifest. Look, I have his papers."

"Well, put him away or something," the flight attendant said, which was totally against procedure. Didn't he know the point of emotional support dogs is that they *be held*? I looked at his badge to tell Flo about him, and I saw that his badge identified him as Brighton McPherson, qualified as a German interpreter.

It would not have caught my attention except that I'd met Brighton McPherson once. He jumpseated next to me across the Midwest a week ago. He spent the entire taxi complaining to me about his boyfriend, who had taken to placing his beloved ancient cat in the storage compartment under the apartment complex while Brighton was away on his trips. I counseled him as best I could, giving him the advice I'd heard my mother dole out on occasion. I've found it works as a universal response to almost all relationship complaints.

"Kick him in the crotch, the bastard," I suggested.

Brighton laughed. "Honey, I will have to try that."

We sat in the rear galley of a 767, and I helped him study for his German-language requalification exam. I love helping flight attendants study for their qualification tests. There are tons of different kinds, be it a foreign-language designation or, my favorite, the annual recurrent training. In Brighton's case, he had key cards with the pertinent airline phrases/questions written on one side and their German translations/answers on the other.

"Why can't passengers use their cell phones while the plane is on the tarmac or during takeoff?" I read from the stack of cards. Brighton responded with a slew of guttural-sounding words that I assumed translated to "because the radio waves can interfere with the cockpit communication," since that is the official answer to that question. I say "official" as opposed to "correct," because I think the correct answer is actually that it's best to pay the hell attention during takeoffs and landings, because that is when crashes are most likely to occur.

Anyway, the Brighton McPherson I knew had blond hair and brown eyes, and this one, while matching the general characteristics of the picture on his badge, had blue eyes. I could tell because when his pupils constricted like they were right now, I saw the real color of his irises rimming the interior of his dark contacts. I guess it was possible for two people in the same department of the same company the size of WorldAir to have the same exact name—in fact there are three (*three!*) flight attendants named Kate Hicks in the trip bidding system alone—but usually the names were common.

I found it pretty doubtful there would be two Brighton McPhersons in the same department, and even more doubtful they would have the exact same employment date and foreign-language designation. Also, there was the matter of Jalyce Sanders, whose true fate had yet to make itself known as far as I could ascertain from Google searches, so this guy would not be the first WorldAir imposter I'd encountered recently, and I say that as one myself.

"*Fuessgelenke umklammern,*" I said to him. I don't really speak German, but I can shout crash commands in three languages. What I actually told this imposter translated to "grab your ankles." It's what the crew is supposed to yell at the passengers in the event of an "unanticipated landing," which is just a euphemistic way to say "crash." Again, I really hate euphemisms. They should just say it like it is. "We're crashing, put your heads down!" or something. Not just "grab your ankles!"

"*Schnauze, Dumkopf,*" he responded. *Hmm*, I thought. *I think he just told me to shut up.* So he either really spoke German, or, like me, he simply memorized some airline phrases to make it appear like he could.

"*Es ist eine Bombe an Bord,*" I countered. It was another foreign-language phrase commonly memorized by rote by those in the industry. It means there's a bomb on board. Its very utterance should strike panic in a flight attendant.

Technically it was the second bomb threat of my career, and it should have elicited mayhem, which I planned to diffuse by deflecting blame and claiming my words were merely misunderstood. Malcolm would have totally backed me up. Oddly, though, this flight attendant simply eyed me levelly and walked away. And the weirdest part is that I could have sworn he understood me.

"What was that about?" Malcolm inquired, returning Captain Beefheart to my arms.

I didn't answer him. I had a decision to make. Should I bring the imposter to the attention of the rest of the crew? Often these charades are carried out with the full knowledge of the parties involved. For all I knew, this guy wearing Brighton's badge was Brighton's coworker or gay lover and he was here to work a shift for him. I didn't want to get a fellow flight attendant in trouble. And I counted myself among them because I did feel a camaraderie to the profession. I had been impersonating my own mother on and off for months, but only as a nonrevenue or jumpseating passenger. You didn't see me walking the aisles and bossing unaccompanied minors around. Not unless it was something Flo expressly asked me to do, which was hardly ever.

Flo was in the lower galley checking the catering supplies as the ground crew boarded them on the plane. Or, more likely, she was chugging a Bloody Mary and signing off on everything with a toast of her thermos. The imposter should have been down there with her as a galley assist, but Flo had probably sent him back up. She liked to work alone on account of how she routinely broke about a dozen federal regulations per flight leg, and you never knew if a coworker would react favorably to that or not.

So I finally decided the best course of action was to quickly sneak down to the lower galley to get Flo's opinion on the event unfolding above her. We had ten minutes before departure, and I had handed Beefheart back to Malcolm and was halfway out of my seat when suddenly the captain announced they were ready to close the forward door and push back from the gate, so could the last trickle of passengers please move their butts and buckle up? Not in those words, but definitely in that spirit.

Dang! I thought. They were departing early because all the passengers were on board and accounted for, though obviously not all were in their seats. A jumble of them were stuck behind a large Hawaiian lady with her hair in a bun almost as big as Flo's. This flight was a through-flight from Grand Cayman as well as a popular East-Coast connection to Honolulu through Los Angeles, so it attracted a lot of vacationers, many of whom had already begun their revelry in the concourse bar before departure. In fact, one of the reasons the Hawaiian lady was having trouble situating herself was because a guy appeared to have passed out, a state which caused him to hog not only his middle seat, but her aisle seat as well.

"Check out the drunk," I snickered, nudging Malcolm.

"What a douche," he said derisively. Malcolm does not take kindly to drinkers, seeing as how his mother is a "volcanic alcoholic," as he put it. I've met her only once myself, and I wisely never bring it up to Malcolm. She reminded me of that training video flight attendants are supposed to watch in order to learn about hypoxia, which is what happens to you when the oxygen masks drop during a decompression and you take your sweet time securing one over your nose and mouth. In short, your brain gets deprived of oxygen and you start acting like you've been exposed to a nerve-gas experiment or something. But the interesting thing about hypoxia is that, evidently, you think you're perfectly fine.

You have no idea that your brain is undergoing total decline. As far as you know everything is hunky-dang-dory.

The training video I'm talking about is an old black-and-white reel that depicts an experiment in which a woman is asked to enter an airtight chamber where scientists observe her through a window. Then they slowly deplete the oxygen from inside the chamber while asking her via intercom to perform a litany of mundane tasks. She gamely complies, thinking she's passing everything with flying colors, when actually she looks like she's swatting at invisible insects the whole time.

Then the scientists ask her to apply a fresh coat of lipstick. She's happy to do it, and commences smearing the stuff all over her face like a toddler with a jar of jam. When she's released from the chamber it takes probably a second for her to revert to normal, and the scientists ask her how she thought she did. She replies that she thinks she did really well. Then they direct her to a mirror where she gets to see her crazy clown face, and everybody laughs and slaps their knees, it's so funny. Har.

The moral of the story is that hypoxia creeps up on you super-fast, *and you have no idea*. That is why, during the in-flight safety demonstrations, the flight attendants always tell you to put the oxygen mask over yourself before helping a child. Because you're not really gonna be all that useful to anyone if you're thinking everything's hunky-dang-dory when really you're just smearing lipstick on your face like a crazy clown.

Regarding Malcolm's mom, it happened some months ago in the WorldAir Flight Club lounge in the F Concourse of the Atlanta airport. The Flight Club lounge is like a giant velvet-rope room for WorldAir's rich zillion-milers. It turns out to be a great place to hang out when you are on the run, especially the one at the Atlanta airport because it has a locker room where you can shower. My ability to sneak into the lounge came about unexpectedly. First, I found that if I hung out directly outside the lounge I could use their free WiFi signal to schedule myself on flights with my iPad. So that was my habit until one day one of the specialty agents inside the lounge came out to tell me my big brother was looking for me, so I'd better get myself inside ASAP.

I had no idea what he was talking about because, for one, I don't have a brother, big or otherwise. And any way you look at it, every family member I have is a WorldAir employee, and WorldAir employees are seriously not allowed to go into the ritzy Flight Club lounges for fear we'd sully the atmosphere with our blue-collaredness. But this agent was certain someone inside was demanding my presence, so I meekly followed him through the door. He led me straight to the back of a plush egg-shaped chair, the kind that evil supervillains sit in, and just like almost all famous scenes with the evil supervillain, the chair swiveled around to face me.

"Malcolm!" I squealed. As ever, I was immensely happy to see him.

"Yes, my dear," he said in his best evil supervillain voice. He held Beefheart in his lap and stroked his head. "Mwaaa ha ha!"

He had seen me sitting on the concourse through the lounge's glass door and instructed the agent to summon me. (He actually used that word, "summon." He cracks me up.) It turned out (of course) that we were scheduled on the same flight to LAX that day, which didn't leave for, like, *hours*.

"Why are you at the airport so early?" I asked. I knew why I was there, as I pretty much lived at airports by that point.

"My mom loves the Flight Club—free booze," he responded, indicating a woman sitting at the bar. She wore her hair like Lucille Ball: flaming red and fluffed like a forties pinup. Her outfit was a bedazzled leopardskin caftan over black leggings. Her shoes were ballet flats encrusted with sharp silver and gold studs at the toes. To be fair, her shoes looked comfortable, and they were in style, if you were to believe the magazines I'd pil-fered from people's seat pockets on occasion. But still, you know . . . wow. She looked to be a Botoxed forty-five years old and about five cocktails to the wind, judging from how she kept rest-ing her head in the crook of her elbow as she raised her empty glass to signal a refill.

"Oh. 'Kay," I said, trying to sound totally accepting. Because I was not one to throw stones, *at all*. Case in point: My mom was in a nut house, my real dad was dead, and my stepdad was a socio-path. Add to that the fact that my best friend in the world was a sixty-seven-year-old cigarette-addicted, booze-addled, old-school stewardess named Flo, and what you have is someone who was living in the most major of glass houses. Seriously.

"She looks nice," I added.

"We definitely see that differently," Malcolm said. "But it's kinda cool I get to finish my homework while watching the planes take off."

Malcolm was referring to our school. I had already mostly completed the online assignments, so I helped him with his. "I have to pick two more people I admire in order to finish my composition," he grumbled, "it might take a few years." I laughed and told him I *totally* sympathized. Then his mother came stumbling over.

"Malcolm, darling, who's this?" she asked, swaying as she stood. She repeatedly tried to light her cigarette but failed hilari-ously until finally one of the lounge attendants came to her rescue and lit it for her.

"She's my friend," Malcolm said, his head down.

I stood and presented her with my hand. "Hello, Ms. Colgate. So nice to meet you. I'm April Manning."

She ignored my hand and redirected her gaze to Malcolm. "I asked you who she is."

"She's my friend," he repeated.

Ms. Colgate took a long draw on her cigarette, inhaling deeply, then blew out the smoke like a makeup-encrusted dragon. "You don't have friends," she slurred, then turned unsteadily on the heel of her weaponized ballet flats and lurched back to the bar.

"Lovely lady," I chirped, practicing my perkiness.

"Right," Malcolm said, then he took my hand. "Come with me," he directed, picking up Captain Beefheart, who grunted adorably like a little sea lion. Malcolm led me to the welcome counter and instructed the agent there to put me in the system as his guest.

"We'll need to have your parent authorize this," the agent told him.

"Fine," said Malcolm. "That's my mother over there." He pointed toward the bar. "I recall you've had the pleasure of speaking to her today on a few occasions already. My ears have almost stopped ringing from that. Let's just call her over here to talk to you again, shall we?"

The agent went pale. "Why, uh, of course we can update your account without having to bother your mother, sir. Let's just make sure I have all your young friend's information in our records here . . . ."

And right there I became a Flight Club member. I tell you it's been a lifesaver, literally. WorldAir has Flight Club lounges in airports all over the globe, but for my purposes, the clubs in the hub airports like Atlanta, Detroit, Chicago, and Los Angeles have been practical domiciles for me lately. I can shower, sleep, and drink all the free sodas I want while waiting for my next flight.

Sometimes I can sneak Flo in with me. The only thing is that she has to be out of her uniform. But she is happy to temporarily slip into her layover clothes for the chance at a free bar before takeoff.

"This certainly takes the bite out of clocking in," she'll joke, belting back a shot of vodka, otherwise known as an "abbreviated Bloody Mary" in Flo's dictionary of cocktail terms.

Until recently I'd been at a loss as to why she hadn't been flagged for a Breathalyzer test following one of her flights, but then I found out one of her ex-husbands is in charge of the facility contracted to administer the (supposedly) random Breathalyzing of airline personnel, and, well, I don't have to say anything further about that. Just suffice it for me to repeat that all four of Flo's known ex-husbands remain devoted to her. Drug tests, though, are a different matter, which is why she pegged me to supply clean urine samples should that need ever arise. Thank God it never has.

Anyway, regarding the WorldAir Flight Clubs, the snack buffets and espresso machines alone kept me alive over the last few months. If not for this development I doubt I could have lasted as long on the run as I have.

But back to Malcolm's mom and how she made me think of the lady in the hypoxia-awareness video. When I saw her with him at the departure gate later, she acted as though everything was hunky-dory, like she'd never seen me before, like she'd never stumbled around and insulted her lovely son as though her brain was being starved of oxygen. She simply handed Malcolm off to the gate agent like he was nothing but a breathing relay baton, then ambled off as though anything in the world was more important than the boy she'd just left behind.

Plus, her lipstick was all askew.

Kowalski:

Kid, c'mon. Get to the part where you break every aviation law in the book.

April Manning:

I am, believe me. But I was told to be as detailed as possible. See? I'm just trying to cooperate.

Kowalski:

All right. Resume.

April Manning:

Like I said, I try not to judge. But because of Malcolm's aversion to drinkers, I always tried to keep his interactions with Flo to a minimum, because Flo, it turned out, had a very low tolerance for people who have low tolerances for drinkers. Whether Flo herself was an actual alcoholic or not was still up for debate, as far as I was concerned. I looked up the list of symptoms on the Internet and they seemed pretty sweeping, in my opinion.

In order to deal with the drunk slumped onto the seat that belonged to the large Hawaiian lady, the imposter Brighton McPherson was summoned from the mid galley to help. It was necessary to get the Hawaiian lady situated so that the others standing in the aisle behind her could get to their seats.

"Again, ladies and gentlemen," the pilot announced over the PA, "we are ready to push back from the jetway just as soon as everyone is seated."

I bet the pilots were motivated to get a move on because World-Air had just ranked fourth before last in this year's *Condé Naste Traveler* list of on-time airlines, and to actually leave early for once was probably a juicy prospect to them. But before they could close the boarding door to the aircraft, they had to make sure all passengers were seated. The incident with the drunk guy was ticking away their head start.

The imposter had made his way aft very reluctantly, if you ask me, which I found curious, because Flo always said the favorite aspect of any flight attendant's job was to throw drunks off the plane. It's ironic, I know. It's like they don't want anyone having more fun than they can.

Finally the Hawaiian lady was just directed to take a different seat, as a number were open, and when she moved out of the aisle I was able to get a look at the passengers in the aisle behind her, and—*Jesus God Christ on the Cross*, I panicked—there stood Ash Manning and his murdering little lizard of a girlfriend.

I ducked my head below the seat in front of me. I was pretty certain they hadn't seen me. I pretended to smooch Captain Beefheart so Malcolm wouldn't think I was nuts, but he didn't fall for it.

"What're you doing?" he whispered.

"That's my stepfather in the aisle up there by the drunk dude, with his girlfriend the Crypt Keeper," I whispered back.

"Whoa!" he exclaimed. "Are you kidding me? I know that woman. She was my guardian ad litem!"

"Serious?"

"As a cyanide pill!"

No wonder his GAL seemed every bit as revolting as mine. They were the same person. "What are they doing?" I asked. "Are they seated yet?"

"No, they're coming this way," said Malcolm, who'd been well (but not thoroughly) briefed on my feelings about these two. "Keep your head down."

"Aren't you afraid she'll recognize you?" I asked.

"Are you kidding? She saw me *once*. In her report to the judge, she described me as wall-eyed and mildly retarded!"

So I did as Malcolm said, and the two of them passed us by, circled via the cross aisle at the back of the cabin and walked up the other side all the way to first class. I ventured a peek as they walked by, and noticed that Ash carried Kathy's giant purse for her. I rolled my eyes. There must not have been enough overhead space in first class, I surmised, which was why they had to bring their bags to the coach cabin.

I considered running off the plane in a mad dash, but then I calmed myself with the knowledge that the front of the plane rarely knew what was happening at the back. One time Flo made it all the way to her layover hotel in Frankfurt before she found out that a man had died of a heart attack in the forward cabin on her flight over.

"I was in the back, separated by three hundred passengers," she justified. "Though I did wonder why it took so long for all the passengers to disembark," she added, chuckling through the smoke of her perpetual menthol.

"Coast is clear," said Malcolm, and nudged me. "You can sit up now."

I breathed a sigh of relief and straightened myself in my seat, just in time to make eye contact with Officer Ned. "Oh, *dang*," I gasped.

"What? What is it?" Malcolm asked.

So this was how I missed seeing two last-minute passengers board the plane. The drunk guy, the large Hawaiian lady, my stepfather, and his evil insect of a girlfriend—all of this created a perfect storm, if you will, to dampen my "situational awareness," which the handbook instructed us to sharpen.

Good situational awareness would be like how, when we board a plane, we're supposed to count the rows to the nearest exit (done), assess escape avenues (done), identify the location and viability of the emergency equipment (done), ascertain the presence of probable imposter flight attendants (done), avoid any proximity whatsoever to known killers in magenta lipstick carrying Louis Vuitton bags, their lapdog boyfriends and/or former stepfathers, as well as any grumpy LEOs who were already half onto me (dang, dang, and *dang*!).

At this point I figured it was time to finally come clean to Malcolm and tell him about my current status as a bona fide runaway. He knew enough from our many past conversations to understand what life for me was like as a nonrev unaccompanied minor, so I didn't have to take twenty years to explain it.

"Won't the airline figure it out?" was all he asked.

"Doubtful," I answered.

It's like when you run a red light, I explained. The police don't sit in front of the red light, they sit behind it, and can only bust you after you've made the transgression. The World-Air pass-travel department is like that policeman, if his job were not to sit right there on the other side of the traffic light, but to sit in a darkened room sifting through miles and miles and miles of surveillance footage looking for red-light runners, and only if he was directed to look for a specific one. In all it meant that maybe, *maybe*, years from now, my mother might get a note in her inbox that read, "What's up with all the non-rev traveling during your family medical leave back in 2013?" or some such.

Seriously, there's something to be said about red tape: it makes a great cloak.

"You can relax now," Malcolm said. "Everything's okay."

"Really?" I asked, lifting my head. Officer Ned was two rows away, stomping toward us, his eyes boring down on me like beams of a red laser.

"*I thought you said everything was okay!*" I slugged Malcolm.

"It will be," Malcolm assured, but his assurance really seemed empty right then. "Seriously, what can he do?"

I started to wonder the same thing—because to be truthful, a part of me was happy to see Officer Ned—when suddenly he was looming over my seat, snorting fire, every breath of which seemed to expand his air of intimidation. I shrank down and peered up at him, trying to seem simultaneously pathetic and innocent as I could.

"April! You, young lady," Officer Ned boomed, his forefinger darting at me, "have some explaining to do. I don't know what you're up to, but I plan to find out. Don't think for a second you're walking off this plane without talking to me."

"Officer, I—" Malcolm tried to interject. I was warmed by how he meant to defend me, but Malcolm wasn't as versed as I was in the depth of unimportance given to anything an unaccompanied minor might have to say.

"Who are you?" Officer Ned bellowed at him, causing not just Malcolm but everyone a few rows surrounding us to cringe. "Scratch that. I don't care. You, April," he pointed at me sharply, "we have business. Do you hear me? Don't you dare move during this flight."

"*Ladies and gentlemen*," the coordinating flight attendant admonished over the PA. "We are on an active taxi. Please take your seats, or I will have to instruct the pilot to stop the aircraft." Since Officer Ned was the only passenger standing, it was obvious to whom the admonishment was directed.

Flo had finished her preflight duties and had come up to take her jumpseat opposite the little elevators that led to the lower galley. But before she did so, she noticed Officer Ned standing in the aisle. She made her way down the aisle toward us as she adjusted the straps to her apron.

"Hey, 'scuse me, Thor," she said to Officer Ned (Flo called all tall, muscular men Thor), "but you have to get your butt in your seat or we can't depart."

"I'm a LEO," Officer Ned tried to clarify. "I just need—"

"I don't care if you're the goddamn Prince of Persia," Flo fumed. "Go back to your seat or I'll tell the pilot to go back to the gate and yank your shapely ass off the plane. Do you get me?"

"I, uh . . . ." Officer Ned's air of intimidation seemed to pop like a party balloon. Flo, though half his size, had a way of sucking the fight out of people. I'd seen her do it many times. She called it "verbal judo," but I don't think there was any real method to it. She was just a worldly sixty-seven-year-old flight attendant who had seen everything, survived it, and didn't scare easily.

"Go on, now," Flo told him. "Sit!"

Officer Ned took a step back, flustered about what to do next. It was like he was being bitten to death by a butterfly.

"Ma'am, I . . . ." he attempted.

"Scoot!" Flo shouted. Officer Ned jumped, turned on his heel, and hightailed it back to his seat to the soft applause of the passengers around us. Flo followed him up the aisle and reminded him to bring his seat back all the way upright. He tried once again to argue, seeing as how he was a hundred feet tall (six-foot-five, I know) and could hardly fit without angling his seat back, but Flo was having none of it, so he obediently complied.

"Wow," Malcolm sighed. "That was something to see."

"That's my friend Flo. You've met her, remember?" I ventured. I wanted to go in baby steps with these two.

"How can I forget?" he asked. I took it as a good sign that he gazed at her with admiration, as I knew for a fact that Flo was probably four Bloody Marys to the wind right then. Maybe these two could tolerate each other after all, I thought.

"Flight attendants, please prepare for departure and cross check," the coordinator instructed over the PA, and with that we backed away from the gate, taxied to the head of the tarmac runway, and took off.

I think about that moment a lot, because if I had gotten a good look earlier at the prisoner Officer Ned was escorting, maybe things would have turned out differently. Maybe I could have employed a diversionary tactic to bring the aircraft back to the gate. God knows I'm capable.

But like I said, my situational awareness had been compromised by the distraction of surrounding events. So when the plane had reached a comfortable cruising altitude and the fasten-seatbelt sign was turned off, and when Officer Ned had arisen to allow his handcuffed prisoner access to the restroom at mid galley . . . I'm haunted by that prisoner's face and how things might have turned out differently if only I'd seen it earlier.

Because I knew that face. I'd seen it last when he broke down the door to Ash's condo, grabbed me by the hair, dragged me out of the house, and threw me in the trunk of his car.

CHAPTER 7

I focused on my breathing because I'd heard doing that can calm your anxiety. Surprisingly, it kinda worked, and by the time Old Cinderblock left the lavatory I had almost finished hyperventilating. He didn't show any signs of recognizing me, which was understandable because of those thick glasses. Beside me, Malcolm was engrossed flipping through the music on his iPad, so he didn't notice my panic.

Old Cinderblock and Officer Ned were seated at 32A and 32B, the two seats along the window on the pilot's side of the plane. This meant they were seated with their backs to the mid galley. *That's a break*, I thought.

"Ladies and gentlemen, once again, welcome aboard World-Air flight 1021, L-1011 jet service to Los Angeles, California," the flight attendant announced over the PA system. "The captain has indicated that you are now able to use your electronic devices, though the seatbelt sign is still illuminated, so please stay seated with your seatbelts securely fastened.

"Also," she continued, "we'd like to extend our congratulations to a pair of newlyweds on board today! WorldAir's own pilot Ash

Manning just married WorldAir's own Kathy Landry, and today they are on their way back from their honeymoon in the Cayman Islands!"

An anemic spattering of applause rippled through the cabin as I tried to suppress my gag reflex. This could not be good.

"Malcolm," I said, but then realized he had his headphones on and was listening to Frank Zappa. "Malcolm," I hissed, yanking the headphones off his ears.

"What?"

"Hand me your notebook, please, and a marker."

He did as I asked. I opened his notebook to a clean page, scribbled a message, and tore the page off. I put the marker in my bag and turned back to Malcolm.

"Now listen to me, and please don't ask questions," I began. I appreciated how his green eyes focused on me with concern. It was so nice to have someone simply believe what I had to say, as opposed to the normal response of the jaded populace (minus LaVonda). "Gather up Captain Beefheart," I instructed, "and follow me."

He did as I said without hesitation. I wanted to kiss him. I grabbed my backpack from underneath the seat in front of me, left the note on my seat, and led him toward the back of the plane and through the aft cross-aisle, then up the opposite aisle to the mid galley. Flo had already descended the elevator to the lower galley, and the imposter Brighton McPherson was retrieving the prepared carts she was sending up to him from below.

"There are five other lavatories at the back," offered one of the flight attendants. She was a tall, heavyset brunette in her late thirties with deep dimples on each cheek when she smiled. Her name badge identified her as Alba Madison, but I knew her as Alby. We'd sat next to each other as nonrev passengers a few months prior. She was in her third year of law school and had given me a sympathetic ear and some sound advice regarding my mother's custody trial. I could tell she didn't place me right away, and I debated refreshing her recollection.

"Hi, Alby, it's April," I said. Oh, what the hell.

She clapped her hand over her mouth in surprise. "Why hi, honey! I'm so sorry I didn't recognize you right away! But can you blame me? Look at you! Your hair and face, all done up. Don't you look all grown-up with those black slacks and white blouse? You almost look like one of us. Don't walk up and down the aisle too much or people will start demanding drinks from you!"

I blushed as she fussed over me for a bit, then I introduced her to Malcolm.

"It might be easier for you to use the lavs in the back," she repeated to him, as the ones near where we stood were being blocked by the flight attendant activities.

"Um, Malcolm needs to use this lavatory because it's the only one with a diaper changing table," I said, indicating Beefheart. This didn't make much sense at all. Beefheart was not only not a baby, but he wasn't wearing diapers, either, dirty or otherwise.

Luckily flight attendants are a pretty accepting bunch. If, for whatever reason, this boy needed the special lavatory with a drop-down changing table for his emotional support animal, far be it for them to question it. Alby simply smiled brightly and told us they'd be out of our way shortly. Not everybody was on board with that, though.

"Hey, I told you to put that dog away," the imposter Brighton McPherson sneered at Malcolm. Luckily, there was another flight attendant in the galley who recognized the significance of Captain Beefheart's green vest.

"Hey, hey, hold on, Rambo," she interjected, reaching out to pet Beefheart. "That's an emotional support pet. He's on the manifest, see?" She snapped the passenger manifest from a clip between the two elevator doors and showed it to him. "Emotional support pets are allowed outside their carriers."

"Oh," said the imposter Brighton McPherson. "Well, I . . . I didn't know."

"What do you mean, *you didn't know?*" she scolded. Her badge revealed her name to be Ramona Thibodaux. She looked to be in her mid-forties with an explosion of dyed-black hair, fake breasts, and a body like a brick house. It occurred to me that she was the crew coordinator. I remembered from helping Flo and my mother prepare for their recurrent training that the flight attendant coordinator often came back to direct the mid galley on L-1011 aircrafts.

"It's right there in our manual," she reminded the imposter Brighton McPherson. I was starting to love this woman.

"Right, I know, I forgot," he stammered, pulling the plastic sheet off a sleeve of Styrofoam cups before placing them next to the coffee server on top of the beverage cart.

"Maybe if you'd made it to briefing today instead of barely getting here in time for boarding . . . ."

She griped at him some more, then directed her attention to Malcolm. "Okay, darling. You just do what you need to do." She cupped Beefheart's face in her hands. "Ooooh, isn't he the cutest little itty bitty honey bunny butter bottoms *in the whole wide world?*" Then she covered Beefheart's snuffly, gnarly, and decidedly *un*-honey butter bottoms face with kisses. It was official. I loved this woman.

Beefheart wiggled his tail-stub and grunted adorably at Ramona's attention. Malcolm made appreciative noises, as well, and soon the coach-class flight attendants had finished preparing their carts and been dispatched to their respective starting points along the aisles of the aircraft.

The coast was clear, so I grabbed the passenger manifest from its clip and pressed the button to call one of the elevators. The two elevators on an L-1011 are little more than dumbwaiters, really. They're only sixteen inches wide but as deep as a meal cart, so they can accommodate two people (or one cart) at a time. Once inside, the only way they can be operated is by flipping two toggle switches simultaneously. The switches are on either side of the interior, so it's impossible to control it with just one hand. This design was intentional, as a "legacy" of earlier-model L-1011s revealed the propensity for injury when the design was different.

"Ripped her arm clean off," Flo had told me, though I'm sure it was an exaggeration.

So now the toggle switches are located on either wall to ensure that both hands are being occupied inside the elevator when it's in use. This can be overridden by the control panels on the outside, as the flight attendants need to be able to send the meal and beverage carts up and down. The elevators cannot operate at all, though, if either door isn't closed securely.

So, even though the elevators at the mid galley of an L-1011 are made for the tight transport of two people and single service carts, if you're not shy, you can add in one wiggle-butted emotional support animal, if need be.

"This is so *totally awesome*," Malcolm said as we descended. "I can't wait to tell my dad about this."

"Malcolm, you can't tell *anyone* about this!"

"Oh, right."

The elevator didn't descend without warning, so when Malcolm and I, along with Captain Beefheart, made our way into the lower galley, Flo had already doused her cigarette and was screwing the cap back onto her thermos of Bloody Marys when she caught sight of us through the glass window of the elevator access door.

"Oh, what the *hell*?" She rolled her eyes. "I just flushed a perfectly good cigarette, April. You were supposed to wait for me to come get you. What's going on?"

"Flo, let me explain . . . ." I began as I stepped off the elevator, revealing Malcolm and Beefheart behind me.

"Seriously, *what the hell*?" Flo groused. "This is all I need, Boy Wonder and his Underdog. My ass is gettin' fired now. Say goodbye to free flight benefits and forty-six years of pension." She shook her head, tapped another menthol from her pack, and lit it.

"You can smoke down here?" Malcolm asked.

"No," Flo said, drawing deeply on her cigarette.

We stood by the sink at the side of the elevators so Flo could exhale directly into the drain. I asked them to gather close so I wouldn't have to raise my voice over the sound of the engines. As Malcolm suppressed his coughs through Flo's smoke, I told them everything that had transpired over the past two and a half weeks—the kidnapping, Jalyce, the escape, the lock-up at the hospital, the escape, Kathy Landry, Old Cinderblock, Officer Ned, the escape, everything—including and up to a few minutes prior, when all the above parties, minus Jalyce but including Ash, had boarded the plane.

When I finished they simply looked at me, as though their minds needed a moment or two to digest what I'd told them. Just as they opened their mouths to pelt me with a million questions, I remembered the imposter Brighton McPherson.

"Oh, and there's an imposter on the plane." I pulled the pairing summary that listed the crew names from my backpack. I like to print them out in the crew lounge or the Flight Clubs before the flights if I can. "The male flight attendant, here, Brighton McPherson. That's not him up there—" I pointed to the cabin above us. "—that's an imposter. I met the real Brighton McPherson a week ago, and that guy up there is not him."

Flo blinked. Malcolm looked like he was still processing everything I'd told him. We all jumped out of our skins when the intercom, which was always set to the highest volume so it could be heard above the engines, buzzed into action: "Trash cart coming down!"

"That's him!" I whispered sharply, indicating the voice on the intercom. "That's the imposter Brighton McPherson."

We jumped again when we heard the loud mechanical churning of the elevator as it made its descent. If there was indeed a cart in there, there would be no room for the imposter, but still Flo directed us to stand flush with the crew luggage shelves behind the jumpseat on the other side of the sink. This kept us from being seen from the vantage of the elevator door as the car made its descent.

"It's too early for them to send down trash carts," I said. "They just started the service."

"I know," Flo said, taking a last drag from her cigarette before dousing it in the sink. "Stay back here, and don't come out unless I tell you."

She went to stand before the elevator door and out of our eyesight. "It's a trash cart all right," she called. I heard her open the elevator door and struggle to pull the cart off the stabling ballast on the elevator car floor. "This is a heavy sucker."

She finally succeeded in pulling it out of the elevator, and I heard her flip open its flat metal lid. "Oh, *what the hell?*"

"What is it?" I jumped out from around the corner, Malcolm and Beefheart at my heels.

"Kids, didn't I tell you to stay back there?" She sounded more concerned than annoyed.

Malcolm obliged politely and returned to his spot, but I continued forward and peered down at the opening on the trash cart lid, then jumped back in alarm.

The opening on the lid didn't provide the greatest view, but it was enough. What I saw was a man's face peering up at me from between his own naked knees. He had been shoved in on his back through the front of the cart, his legs bundled into a fetal position above him. His eyes were open and bulging, his tongue dark and protruding, his lips frozen in a horrific grin of death.

"That's him, Flo!" I gasped, tears welling in my eyes.

"Who?"

"That's the *real* Brighton McPherson!"

CHAPTER 8

"What's that around his neck?" Flo asked.

"It's a garrote," I answered, recognizing the handles at each end of the wire that was still knotted tightly around the dead man's throat. It was either a convenient or a sad fact that my mother's and Grammy Mae's addiction to true-crime television had prepared me with this knowledge.

The terror barely had time to register in either of us before the loud mechanical churning began, indicating one of the elevators was in action again. I scurried back to stand beside Malcolm, who gave me a look that silently begged for an update on recent developments. I cupped one hand over my mouth and the other over his, then put my palms together in a praying position to try and impart the importance of staying silent right then. He understood. Beefheart, as ever and thank God, rested in his arms, as calm as a monk.

I heard Flo flip the lid of the trash cart closed just as the elevator engine stopped and its door opened.

"I need you to stand over here," the voice said. He was no longer trying to fake a Southern accent, but I could tell it was the imposter Brighton McPherson.

"Scooter," Flo said (she called all men who were thin and well-groomed Scooter), "I need you to shove this trash cart straight up your puckered poo hole."

I could feel my senses heighten, remembering another list my mother had given me that I kept tucked in my flight attendant manual:

Mom's List of Five Great Make-Do Weapons on an Aircraft

1. **Another passenger's aluminum crutch or cane.** Two presumed hijackers were beaten to death with one of these on a Chinese flight last year.
2. **The red Halon fire extinguisher.** There is always at least one of these on board, usually mounted on the bulkhead behind the last row of seats in each cabin. It's heavy and metal and can drop you like a mofo if you're hit with it.
3. **The H_2O fire extinguisher.** There is also always at least one of these on board, too, right next to the red one. It's smaller, but even heavier because it's filled with water instead of Halon gas.
4. **The liquor kit.** All those booze minis come in a long metal sleeve that slides in and out of the beverage cart. Yank that out and swing it around hard enough and heads will (probably) literally roll.
5. **Can of soda.** These suckers are heavy, and if you throw one hard enough it can be like a big, slow bullet to someone's head.

I had just unclipped the H$_2$O fire extinguisher from its bracket by the jumpseat when I heard the imposter yell to Flo, "Do as I say, old lady!"

I jumped out just as the man jumped over the cart, which Flo had positioned as a block between her and the elevator, and caught her neck in another of his garrotes. Without hesitation, I clouted him across the back of the head with the thin metal tank as hard as I could.

"What the . . . *ouch!*" He clutched his head and turned to face me.

Surprisingly, the blow didn't knock him out, but at least he dropped his grip on the handles of the garrote. This freed Flo to pull it from her neck and gasp air into her lungs. By then the imposter had turned his attention to me. I swung the extinguisher into his gut battering ram–style, but the only purpose it seemed to serve was to make him more furious, if that was possible.

The look on his face pierced a million little icicles of fear into my heart. His teeth were bared like a hyena, his eyes monstrous in their anger. I tried to hit him with my weapon again, but he was too close; in fact he was coming at me with the force of a freight train.

"April, duck!" I heard Flo call out.

I covered my head with my arms and dropped to the floor just as I heard a curious popping sound. The imposter hit the ground in front of me like a sack of wet cement. His arms grazed mine as he fell.

For a moment everything was silent but for the roaring of the engines, then I stood up and assessed the condition of the assailant. His head was bleeding, and he was not moving. I backed away and looked at Flo with confusion.

"What did you hit him with?" I asked.

"A bullet," she said. "That'll be the last time that bastard ever calls me 'old lady.'"

CHAPTER 9

"Flo! What are you doing with a gun?" I exclaimed. She placed the gun on the counter and sifted through her carry-on bag, which, judging by how most of the contents were strewn at her feet, must have been where she normally kept it.

"I always carry one." She found the lighter she was looking for and lit another cigarette. The quaking of the flame echoed the shaking of her hands.

"You can't bring a gun on an aircraft!"

"Says who?"

"Says security!"

"I don't carry it through security," she said.

"Wait . . . what?"

"We're picked up at the employee parking lot and brought straight to the crew lounge under the concourse. I can bring anything on board I want." Her shaking had subsided, and I gave her a big hug.

It was starting to make sense. Flo worked high-time turnarounds, like this one to LAX and back. Her "layover" consisted of fifty minutes at the gate. She never left the plane, let alone went outside security. *She can bring anything on board she wants.*

Malcolm finally made a sound. "What about decompression?"

"What?" Flo and I asked at the same time.

"The bullet could have ricocheted and caused an explosive decompression? Like what happened on that Aloha Airlines flight in the late eighties," Malcolm recited, "when a crack in the fuselage caused the front end of the plane to rip open midflight and suck out a flight attendant right along with her beverage cart."

I shook my head. "That was due to the age of the aircraft and stress in the construction, not a bullet hole," I countered. "Didn't you see *Mythbusters*? They tested the bullet-hole theory and found that any extra internal pressure caused by a bullet through the fuselage still wouldn't be enough to cause an explosive decompression."

"Even at cruising altitude?"

"Yeah, I know, right? I was surprised, too."

"All right, Einsteins," Flo interjected, "this is a .22, it's not gonna go through any walls. The shot wasn't even loud enough to be heard over the engines. The bullet didn't even exit the back of that guy's head." She pointed, and we all turned our heads to silently look at the disheveled and dead imposter on the floor.

We jumped when the intercom screeched to life. "Flo, can you send up a few bags of ice and some milk, please?" The voice belonged to Ramona.

Flo grabbed a half dozen small cartons of milk from one of the reach-ins, I grabbed two large bags of ice from the freezer, and we both tossed them in the elevator and pushed the up button.

"Coming right up." Flo spoke into the handset as pleasantly as possible, considering the circumstances. Then she turned back to me and Malcolm.

I furrowed my brow in thought. "Flo, I remember Ramona saying the imposter didn't make it to briefing, right?"

"Right. We had a message on our sign-in screens informing us the pre-flight briefing would be held on the aircraft instead of one of the briefing rooms in the lounge," she answered.

"Well, it looks like the real Brighton McPherson actually did make it to briefing, but then got intercepted," I said.

"I'm calling the pilot," Flo insisted, lifting the handset.

I halted her by placing my hand on her arm and pointing to the manifest I'd brought with me down from the mid galley. At the top of the sheet, someone (presumably Ramona, the coordinator) had inked in the three names of the pilots on duty in the cockpit—as well as a fourth name, the name of the off-duty pilot riding jumpseat in there with them.

That name was Ash Manning.

Flo replaced the handset in its cradle, took her packet of cigarettes out, and lit another one. "What's your suggestion?" she asked.

"Well, we don't know if this guy is the only imposter on the crew," Malcolm offered.

I looked at him. *Impressive*, I thought. "Right! Flo, were there any other flight attendants on the crew that you didn't know or recognize?"

Flo exhaled her smoke dejectedly. "Kid, you know how it is. It's not like it used to be when we all knew each other. There are fifteen thousand flight attendants at WorldAir now, and with trip drops, swaps, and jetway trades, we never know who we're flying with anymore. That's part of the beauty of this job. And it's the reason you've been able to stay on the run for the past few weeks."

"Can you confirm the identity of *anyone* on your cabin crew?" I asked.

"I just drank a thermos of Bloody Marys! I barely recognize *you*!"

"Oh, that's comforting. You just fired a gun in my direction!"

"You should count your lucky stars, normally I'm a *terrible* shot."

"Excuse me," Malcolm interrupted. "I think I have an idea."

We turned to him expectantly.

"Isn't that the stowage area for the crew bags?" he asked, pointing to the shelves on the other side of the sink where he and I had hidden earlier. Black regulation suitcases were stacked one on top of the other on the shelves, secured with a sheet of thick plastic webbing across the alcove to keep them in place.

Yes, we nodded, those were definitely the crew bags.

"Well, let's look through them and see if we can find anything suspicious. Or at least see if any other flight attendant brought a weapon on board today. We could probably use it, the way things are going."

"Good idea," I said. "Flo, why don't you start on that. Malcolm, we need to do something about this . . ." I indicated the dead imposter Brighton McPherson. " . . . this situation."

"You want *me* to . . . ." Malcolm stammered. I knew it was asking a lot. This was probably his first dead body, while I was starting to feel like a freakin' pro.

I nodded sympathetically. "We can't risk him being seen by any of the other crew members until we can rule them out as imposters as well."

Malcolm placed an airline blanket inside the sink and put Beefheart on it with a ramekin of water at his side. He turned to me with an air of readiness, like a butler about to receive my bidding. My heart widened a bit. I was so grateful for his presence, yet so sorry to have involved him in this. We rifled through the dead man's pockets to see if we could find his true identity, but all we found was his cell phone and another one of those plastic devices with a clip on the back that looked like a garage-door opener. It had a screen for a digital display very similar to the one I'd retrieved from the purse

I'd snaked from the trunk of Old Cinderblock's car a few weeks earlier. Kathy's small auxiliary purse.

I grabbed a flight attendant apron, notorious for their deep pockets, and put it on. Once all the pertinent items were transferred from the imposter's pockets to mine, I anchored an empty meal cart near his feet, clicked open its front flap, and we unceremoniously shoved the imposter Brighton McPherson inside of it with all the pomp and tenderness I'm sure he himself had shown to the real Brighton McPherson.

Surprisingly there wasn't much blood spatter, considering this was a crime scene where an assailant had been shot in the forehead. But there were some specks on the wall and a spot about the size of a salad plate that had soaked into the grotty old flooring. Thank God the bullet hadn't exited the back of his skull; it spared us the gore of many of the crime scenes my mom and I had watched together on true-crime television.

As though reading my thoughts, Flo said, "Don't worry about the blood. They never clean these planes. For all the crew cares, that stain is left over from some other accident years ago. Believe me, people are always bleeding in this thing. If you sprayed luminal down here this place would light up like a Jackson Pollack painting."

Malcolm and I both stifled a shudder. I was covering the spot with another airline blanket when suddenly the intercom squawked to life.

"Flo!" Alby's voice blared. "We found a bomb threat on board! Start stowing the carts. We're landing immediately."

"What kind of bomb threat?" Flo asked.

"It's a note. I found it on seat 42B."

"What does it say?"

"It's written in red Sharpie marker. It says, 'There is a bomb on board this plane! Not kidding!'"

CHAPTER 10

"Seat 42B. Got it." Flo turned away from the intercom, crossed her arms, and glared at me sternly. "Care to let me in on this, April?"

"I needed to create a diversion!" I cried. I knew flight attendant protocol dictated that all bomb threats be treated seriously, no matter how trivial they may seem. Standard practice was to alert the other flight attendants and the pilots, and prepare the aircraft for an immediate landing.

"Malcolm, remember that incident in 2009?" I pleaded. "When a passenger found a note in the seat pocket in front of her, and all she had to do was hand it to the flight attendant and they landed the plane right then and there?"

"Totally!" Marcus chimed in. He had begun pulling the crew bags from their shelves and opening them in search of anything useful and/or suspicious.

"Never mind that it was a giant Boeing 747 and the nearest airport was a regional strip that was hardly long enough to land a dragonfly," he continued. "They plunked the plane straight down, overshooting the runway by a hundred yards and deploying the emergency slides and everything. The note was written on a barf bag by a previous passenger. No one knows how previous. It could have been years."

"I know," I joined in. "I loved the simplicity of it. Just one sentence, 'There's a bomb on board,' and *boom!*, mayhem . . . ."

"Mayhem, exactly. Mayhem is a great diversionary tactic."

" . . . except later it was determined to be a bad joke."

"What're you kids, the Psychotic Bobbsey Twins?" Flo grumbled as the carts began their descent in the elevators. "And I think your pet crocodile peed in the sink," she told Malcolm. I helped her as she deftly pulled the carts off their ballasts and rolled them into slots under the rows of convection ovens. I was impressed. Flo weighed ninety-five pounds and I knew for a fact that a full L-1011 beverage cart weighed more than three hundred pounds.

"It's all in the leverage," Flo grunted as though reading my thoughts again. It occurred to me that this was the first time I'd actually seen her work. Wow, she could be a rocket if she put her mind to it.

Malcolm continued to rummage through the crew bags, calling out the items he came across to let us ascertain their potential usefulness:

Curling Iron? Yes.

Hairbrush? No.

Shaving cream? Yes.

Extension cords? *Yes!*

Bible? No.

Swiss Army knife? *Hell yes!*

Four-inch heels? Maybe . . . okay, no.

Hairspray? Yes.

Masking tape? Yes.

Prescription medication?

"What kind?"

"Sectrol . . . ."

"That's a beta-blocker," Flo said.

"Xanax . . . ."

"That's for anti-anxiety."

"Cafergot . . . ."

"That's to treat migraines."

Malcolm stopped digging through the medicine and looked at Flo. "How do you know all this?" he asked.

"That's my bag you have there," she said. I asked her if any of the drugs were deadly. "Not really," she answered, "but I wouldn't recommend taking them all at once. That Cafergot, especially. It can make your brain set off car alarms from across the street."

I directed Malcolm to put the drugs in the "yes" pile of useful things, but not before Flo grabbed a supply from each canister and stuffed them in her apron pocket.

Malcolm went on to the next bag.

"Zip ties," continued Malcolm.

"Wait, whose bag is that?" I asked.

"It doesn't say, there isn't a crew tag on it."

"What else is in it?"

Before Malcolm could answer me, the intercom blared once again.

"False alarm, Flo," Alby's voice carried into the galley. Maybe it was the grinding of the jet engines, but she sounded nervous. "We're not landing after all."

Flo and I looked at each other with misgiving. "Ah, this is not according to protocol," Flo said into the speaker.

"I know. Can you please send up some pepper to put on their eggs."

"Say again?"

"Pepper, for their eggs."

What? I thought. This was an afternoon flight; there weren't any egg dishes on board. There was hardly anything at all on board now that the airlines have cut back their first-class meal service to what was practically a sack lunch. Malcolm looked perplexed as well, but he was looking down into the bag before him rather than at the source of the message.

"What's all this about eggs and pepper?" I asked Flo.

"It means . . ." She tried to act calm as she tapped out another menthol from her diminishing pack, but was betrayed once again by her shaking fingers. "It means," she began again, "that we're being hijacked."

I clapped my hands over my mouth. *Crap!* I should have known. The cabin and cockpit crews always establish a unique code phrase during briefing for exactly this type of situation.

Eggs and pepper. *Duh.*

Hopefully the pilots had been paying attention. They should be privy to all interphone communication between the cabin crew during the flight—like an ongoing party line. For whatever reason, Alby had called us, not the pilots, but surely she was counting on them hearing her.

But again, I have major trust issues, and a large reason is because of pilots. I am not *at all* confident they perform as competently as they should. Ash alone is a walking cautionary tale. He once had to take a month's disciplinary leave because he forgot to lower the landing gear on approach. It wasn't until he got close enough to the landing strip that the tower caught a visual and told him about it. He had to abort the landing and redirect to another airport because he didn't have enough fuel to stay the holding pattern.

And take the story (totally true) about those pilots who fell asleep at the wheel, overshot San Francisco, and were halfway across the Pacific before the flight attendant finally pounded on the cockpit door. And what about that incident in 2010 when two WorldAir pilots mistakenly landed a jet with one hundred and eighty passengers on the taxiway of Minneapolis airport—not the runway, but the *taxiway*. Evidently they'd spent the flight surfing the Internet in the cockpit, and somehow that caused them to forget the difference between an empty runway and a taxiway that is anything but empty—usually. Luckily, no one died. Oh my *God,* don't even get me started about the pilot mistakes that result in mass casualties.

Flo placed her hand on my arm because I was starting to hyperventilate again. I looked at Malcolm for support, but he was still peering into the crew bag, his face full of puzzlement. I recognized the candy-colored TSA lock on it that Malcolm had easily picked. *That's Ash's bag*, I realized. I focused on my breathing once more. I'm surprised at how well this works to calm you down.

"Malcolm," I asked when I settled a bit. "What are you looking at?"

He lifted his head to meet my eyes, a look of sheer bewilderment on his face.

"A bomb," he said.

PART VII

THE BOMB

Preliminary Accident Report, cont.
WorldAir flight 1021, April 1, 2013
Present at transcript:
April May Manning, unaccompanied minor
Detective Jolette Henry, Albuquerque Police Department
Investigator Peter DeAngelo, NTSB
Investigator Anthony Kowalski, FBI

Agent Kowalski:
So you're saying . . . .
April Manning:
The bomb wasn't mine.
Investigator DeAngelo:
But the note . . . .
April Manning:
Ironically, the note was. I mean, super ironically. Because of the top ten things I expected to encounter today, I'd say an actual bomb would be in the bottom four. The top six, of course, would include overworked gate agents and a crowded Concourse B at the airport, where the flight to Los Angeles departed from gate number thirty-four, which, wouldn't you know, is the furthest possible gate from the escalator. It is like number four on my list of fifty worst airport gates of all time. It's a good thing I don't have any luggage.

Thanks for the blanket, Inspector DeAngelo, it's getting chilly in here.

Agent Kowalski:
Listen, Nancy Drew, I'm finding it hard to believe anything you say. We've got your friend Malcolm in the other room, and he's telling us a different story. He's dropping the dime on you as we speak.

April Manning:
Agent Kowalski, you and I see things a lot differently. For example, I know you're lying to me about Malcolm.

Investigator DeAngelo:
Kowalski, I told you that wouldn't work.
Agent Kowalski:
Listen to me! We've got three dead bodies . . . .
April Manning:
Four.
Agent Kowalski:
. . . *four* dead bodies . . . .
April Manning:
At least.
Agent Kowalski:
. . . at *least*, and one of them is my informant. I need to get to the bottom of this.
Inspector DeAngelo:
Then let her finish, Kowalski! April, what about the bomb?
April Manning:
Right, the bomb. The bomb appeared to be a basic circuit-board model attached to a plastic explosive inside a boom box. Ironic, huh? *Boom* box? It looked like it could have been the kind that was reportedly used to bomb Pan Am flight 103 over Locker-bie in 1988. All two hundred seventy people on that plane were killed, you know. Plus a bunch on the ground.
Inspector DeAngelo:
I'm very aware of that. What else did it look like?
April Manning:
The boom box was an old Toshiba model with the big speakers on either side. Malcolm thought it looked weird for three reasons. One, the front panel was removed, exposing a dense block of what looked like off-white Play-Doh at the center between the two speakers. Two, there was a choke collar attached to it by a chain about four inches in length. And three, *who brings boom boxes anywhere anymore*?

Inspector DeAngelo:

True.

April Manning:

Malcolm held the bag with both hands, too frightened to put it down. Flo immediately snuffed out a perfectly good cigarette, which, if you knew Flo, totally confirmed the gravity of the situation.

"What do I do?" Malcolm asked.

"Um, okay, uh," I jabbered, "according to the 'Bomb Recognition' section in the flight attendant manual, the first on the list of things to look for in a suspicious device is, um, an explosive."

"That would be the big chunk of C-4 in the center there, right?" Flo pointed.

"Right. Okay, now where is the power source?"

"Could it be those two big Eveready batteries?" Malcolm squeaked.

"Yes, it definitely could. Very good, Malcolm." I tried to sound upbeat, and Malcolm actually did crack a weak smile.

"What about an initiator?" Flo asked, eager to interject her training as well. "There's supposed to be an initiator, right? Do you see an initiator?"

"Yeah, actually I do," I responded, pointing at it.

"Oh, hell," she sighed.

"I don't see a sensor, though," I informed them.

Malcolm's grip on the bag handles had whitened his knuckles. "What? What does that mean? No sensor?"

"It means what you've got there is a bomb with no on-switch," Flo said. I was impressed. You would have thought she didn't pay attention when I drilled her on this in preparation for her recurrent training each year. "You can put it down, *carefully*."

Malcolm gently placed the bag on the floor, then reached to pick up Beefheart out of the sink and move him away. As the dog passed over the bag, though, a digital panel on the boom box sprung to life and began to beep.

"What the hell?" Flo gasped.

"*Crap!*" I squeaked.

Malcolm clutched Beefheart to his chest and looked stricken. Then he pointed to my pocket. "Why is your pocket glowing, April?" he asked.

Out of nervousness I had been clutching in my pocket the strange device I'd taken from the imposter Brighton McPherson. I pulled it out and saw that the digital window was lit up and scrolling some numbers and letters. The information appeared jumbled but for two unmistakable words. I had to blink my eyes to make sure I was reading them right. To this day I can't believe what they spelled.

Agent Kowalski:

What did they spell?

April Manning:

"Captain Beefheart."

Agent Kowalski/Investigator DeAngelo/Detective Jolette Henry:

What?

April Manning:

I know!

Agent Kowalski:

Lord Jesus Christ on the cross, kiddo! If I find out you're spinning stories and wasting our time I'll throw you in a damp slammer filled with rats, I don't care how too-young you are! This is a serious situation! There are four dead bodies—

April Manning:

At least.

Agent Kowalski:

At least!

Investigator DeAngelo:

Kowalski, stop with the hardball and let her finish her statement. April, what did you do next?

April Manning:

Flo took the device from my hand and said, "This looks like the thing the vet used to read the microchip on my fourth husband's pit bull. Her name was Fifi Trixabelle, and it showed up on the reader just like that one does."

"Your fourth husband had a pit bull named Fifi Trixabelle?" Malcolm asked.

"Sweetest thing you ever saw. Wish I'd gotten custody of her in the divorce."

I walked across the galley and the scanner stopped glowing. More importantly, the bomb stopped beeping. I took the batteries out of the scanner, put them in my pocket, placed the scanner in the stowage compartment furthest from the crew bag, and clicked it shut. Then finally I spoke.

"Guys," I said, "I think we found the bomb's on-switch."

"Is it that scanner?" Malcolm gasped.

"No, the scanner only activates the sensor."

"Then what's the sensor, kid?" Flo's voice was getting hoarse from lack of nicotine.

"It's Beefheart. He's the sensor! That collar is for him!" I pointed to the choke collar attached to the boom box. It was one of those particularly nasty kinds of choke collars, with vicious spikes lining the interior meant to inflict maximum pain on the animal. "And look at the digital read on the boom box," I continued. It had begun to show numbers rapidly counting down, then stopped. "If this thing starts up again, we have less than *one hour.*"

Malcolm shook his head briskly, in complete disbelief. "This makes no sense," he insisted. "How can Beefheart . . . he can't be . . . this makes no sense."

Flo instinctively took out her pack of menthols, then remembered the bomb, cursed under her breath and handed the cigarettes and lighter to me, presumably to allay any force of habit.

"Look, Malcolm." I rummaged through my backpack and pulled out the piece of notebook paper I'd taken from Kathy's purse after she and Cinderblock murdered Jalyce. Kathy's pterodactyl scratchings didn't make much sense to me at the time, but now things were starting to clarify. "See this paper, it's Kathy's writing, right there it says 'angels,' and those scribbles next to it? They say 'among us.'"

"Angels among us," Malcolm recited. Realization was starting to descend upon his features, but Flo was still completely in the dark.

"What?" she insisted. "What the hell does that mean?"

I took Beefheart's certification papers from a slot on his vest and unfolded them. "Look," I pointed. "Angels Among Us is a pet-rescue organization based in Georgia. They cherry-pick dogs from among their strays to send off and be trained as emotional support dogs—it's an experimental program put together by the Fulton County Penitentiary. Before they're certified, these dogs spend months in the possession of prison inmates."

Malcolm tightened his embrace around Beefheart. I didn't blame him. Beefheart grunted sweetly, licked his master's face, and wriggled his tail stub. I choked back a sob.

"We have to tell the pilots," Flo said.

"If we're being hijacked, how do we know who's really flying the plane?" I reasoned. "Remember, Alby called *us* to give the code word. Not the pilots."

"Then who do we tell?" Flo asked.

I furrowed my brow thoughtfully, then shook my head in resignation.

"What?" Malcolm asked. "Who do we tell?"

"Officer Ned," I said.

CHAPTER 11

I took out the imposter's cell phone and punched in the contact number from the business card Officer Ned had given me what seemed like a century ago. It rang four times and then went to voicemail. I left a synopsized message detailing the day's events as briefly as I could. Then I hung up and tried again. Straight to voicemail. Dang. Wouldn't you know he'd probably be the only one who actually turned off his phone during flight.

So it was on to Plan B.

An L-1011-250 model with a lower galley like this one is designed with a hatch in the cabin floor near the mid galley. Flight attendants are trained to use this hatch in case the elevators stop working. A good thing about this hatch is that it's flush with the aisle floor and its seams are indecipherable in the thin, grody old seventies carpet that lines the aisles of the aircraft. Many of these hatches have never been opened even once, and after decades of being trampled and spilled on, I was worried we'd be unable to open this one.

But after some rigorous scraping along the edges with the Swiss Army knife, I was able to dislodge enough grime to lift the hatch half an inch to assess the condition of the cabin, or at least the floor of the cabin. Malcolm held me aloft by gripping me around my thighs so that the two of us made a human extension of sorts. The side of his head rested right at my belly.

"Your stomach sure is growling," he said.

"Shut up!" I smacked the top of his head lightly. Once again I was so glad, and simultaneously sorry, that he was here with me.

I was surprised to see the passengers in the cabin behaving as though nothing was wrong. Either they didn't know we were in danger, or Alby's message had been coerced, or worse, duplicitous. There was no sight or sound of any flight attendants nearby, so I took a moment to evaluate the surroundings, as this vantage point proved to be pretty advantageous.

Officer Ned, unmistakably identifiable by his black motorcycle boots, and his prisoner Old Cinderblock had the two window seats directly opposite the hatch on the other side of the aircraft. Directly next to the hatch was a carry-on bag with a box of thin spaghetti peeking above a pocket. I stealthily reached out, took it, and put it in my own pocket. Another nearby passenger had a stack of porno magazines sticking out of his bag. (Really, what is it about porno and airplanes?) Then, a few rows up on the copilot's side of the cabin, I spotted the telltale sign of an ankle holster peeking out from beneath a man's pant leg.

I closed the hatch and whispered to Malcolm to let me down.

"Flo," I said. "The guy on the aisle seat at 29H, did you get a look at him?"

"Are you talking about the air marshal?" she responded.

"Why didn't you tell me there's an air marshal on board?"

"Kid, I would have gotten around to it eventually, but you gotta admit, two dead bodies and a bomb can be pretty distracting."

"How do you know he's an air marshal?" Malcolm asked. "I thought they traveled incognito, even to the flight attendants."

Flo and I chuckled wryly. "They couldn't be easier to identify if they wore a uniform, which come to think of it, they kind of do," Flo explained.

"Yeah," I clarified. "Just picture a Hawaiian shirt on a guy who looks like the last thing in the world he'd ever wear is a Hawaiian shirt."

I put the packet of spaghetti in the pile of useful things Malcolm had culled from the crew bags. He looked at me curiously and asked, "Are we making lunch?" I smiled wanly and asked him to tear me another piece of paper from his notebook. Then I produced the Sharpie marker I'd borrowed from him earlier and wrote a note to Officer Ned. It read:

> *Officer Ned. There is a bomb on the plane. A picture of it is on the cell phone inside the vest pocket. Also, we think we're being hijacked. Please go right now and stand by the lavatory on the other side of the aisle from you.*
>
> *P.S. Please don't show this note to anyone.*
> *P.P.S. This is April.*
> *P.P.P.S. I'm serious.*

Then Malcolm handed over the most precious thing in his life to me. I took Beefheart, tucked the cell phone with the picture of the bomb in the slot on the back of his vest, and put the note in the dog's mouth. Then Malcolm lifted us both up to peek through the hatch again. When I saw that the coast was clear, I widened the opening and placed Beefheart on the floor facing the opposite aisle.

"Boots, Beefheart!" I whispered with the excitement dogs love to hear. "The boots." I pointed. "Go get the boots."

Beefheart wiggled his tail stub eagerly and set off toward Officer Ned's feet. Please, please, Officer Ned, I prayed, please don't be a grump and kick the dog down the aisle or something.

Beefheart padded quietly behind the last row of seats in the mid cabin to get to the opposite aisle, then up a few rows toward Officer Ned. I could hear a few squeals of delight from some surrounding passengers as they caught sight of the small dog, because dogs don't commonly walk the aisles of an aircraft, but that was all. No one created an uproar over pet allergies, like Malcolm and I have seen people react on past flights, thank God. Soon Beefheart reached Officer Ned's boots and began scratching at them softly with his paw.

"C'mon, pick up the dog," I whispered.

The leather on those cowboy boots must have been thick, because it wasn't until the passenger across the aisle pointed it out to him that Officer Ned finally noticed Beefheart. First he petted Beefheart's head, then he must have noticed the note in the dog's mouth, because he reached down to pick him up.

"He got him! He got him!" I whispered excitedly to Malcolm. "He's getting up! He's coming over!" Then I waited, trying to keep the hatch opening as thin as possible. Then, *plunk!*, somebody stepped on the hatch and it thwacked down on my head. Hard.

"*Ouch*," I smarted.

"You okay?" Malcolm asked.

"Yeah." I rubbed my head. "Are you?"

"I'm fine," he answered. He seemed to hold me up effortlessly, the side of his head still snug against my abdomen.

I pushed up on the hatch and it wouldn't budge. It occurred to me that the person who stepped on it was still standing on it. Then it further occurred to me that the person standing on it was Officer Ned.

Flo was one step ahead of me and had already entered the elevator to go up and get him.

"Hey, Thor," I heard Flo call. "This way."

Finally the hatch didn't resist when I pushed up on it. Then I heard the familiar churning of the elevator engine as the car descended, and soon Officer Ned was looking through the small window at us. Fury and worry seemed to fight for the expression on his face. Then Malcolm opened the elevator door, and Officer Ned unfolded his big six-foot-five self from the interior of the tiny elevator, and I immediately noticed two things missing.

"Where's Beefheart?" Malcolm asked.

"Where's Flo?" I asked.

"April, what is going on?" Officer Ned's voice sounded more frantic than mad.

"We only know what we told you in the note," I explained. "Please, where's Beefheart and Flo?"

"Flo is . . . ?" He swirled his hand above his head to indicate Flo's customary large hairdo. I nodded. "And Beefheart is . . . ?" He pinched his ear to indicate Beefheart's lovely little half-chewed-off ear. I nodded. "They're up there. They couldn't fit in the lift with me, so Flo took the dog and said she'd be down right behind me."

Malcolm and I looked at each other in a panic. Where were they, then? Suddenly the second lift churned to life, and we both breathed a sigh of relief. But when the door opened it wasn't Flo after all. It was the coordinator, Ramona Thibodaux. Malcolm and I froze, not knowing what to think or do. She opened the door and smiled so sweetly at me that I felt my tension ease, then she took Flo's gun from her apron pocket, pointed it at my head and fired twice.

PART VIII

THE GUNS

Remember I told you about how Officer Ned chased down that escaped prisoner on the tarmac of the LAX airport? Remember I said I'd never seen anyone move so fast? I didn't think I ever would again—until today in the lower galley of that L-1011 when Ramona Thibodaux pointed a gun at my head. It happened like a shadow, or a flash—a blink, I'm telling you. It was so quick that I wondered where the bullets went, because surely she had hit me, I thought. But no, the bullets didn't hit me. They hit Officer Ned.

He had thrown himself between me and the gun.

Malcolm and I both screamed so loud that we could hear passengers above us start to react in astonishment. The popping sound of gunfire was not startling, because evidently old, rickety airplanes like this one made crazy noises all the time. But screaming, now, that was cause for alarm.

Malcolm ran to me and embraced me. I don't think he understood I hadn't been shot until he held me at arm's length and assessed my condition. Ramona kept clicking the trigger on Flo's gun to no avail. She banged it against the door to see if she could unjam it, then tried shooting it at us again. The gun must have been out of bullets, because she angrily stuffed it in her apron pocket, closed the door of the elevator and began ascending.

I was too stunned from what had transpired to stop her, but Officer Ned, bleeding and by sheer force of will, dragged himself to the elevator door and yanked it open. The car had nearly made it to the top, but not completely. When Officer Ned opened the door, it stopped the car in mid-ascent, exposing Ramona's legs from the knees down. Officer Ned grabbed her ankles and tried to pull her back into the galley. But Ramona kicked like a bronco. Remember, she's built like a brick house, and plus there was someone above who was pulling her up, not to mention the fact that Officer Ned had been shot twice, so in the end we lost that battle, and Ramona clambered up and out of sight, minus both her shoes.

I ran to Officer Ned, who had collapsed and was breathing raggedly. "What do I do?" I asked Malcolm. There was nothing in the first aid section of the manual that told us how to treat gunshot wounds. Officer Ned was bleeding badly. I could feel the panic rise in my chest and the tears well in my eyes.

What do I do what do I do what do I do? Then I heard my mom's voice. *Don't freak out. Figure it out.* I sprang into action.

"Malcolm, get me the first aid kit from above the jumpseat over by the sink. See it there? Good. Now bring me the emergency medical kit from above the other jumpseat on the other side of the elevators. Thanks. Now, grab the defibrillator from the bracket above the cupboard. It's that red square thing with the little blinking lightning bolt by the handle. Good."

From there I worked in a blur as all the training I'd helped other flight attendants study for kicked me into autopilot. A gunshot wound is a wound, after all. I knew how to treat those. As far as I could discern, Officer Ned had been shot in the left arm and in the torso near the right side of his ribs. I pulled off one of his motorcycle boots and, using the scissors in the defibrillator kit, cut off the strap so I could wrap it around his arm to apply pressure and secure the bandage.

Then I directed Malcolm to look into Flo's bag for painkillers, because I knew she must have had some in there. I shook three into my palm and fed them to Officer Ned one at a time, two because he was at least twice her size and one extra because, well, he was shot up. I bundled him in airline blankets and kept the defibrillator at the ready in case he started to die on me. Thankfully he didn't just then, and soon he seemed to be as stabilized as we could hope for considering the situation.

I sat back and exhaled, finally.

But not for long.

I ran to the elevators and banged the buttons to descend the cars so I could ride them up. "April, where are you going?" Malcolm called. We could hear some passengers above us still chattering in the kind of half panic that comes with understanding that things are not right but not knowing exactly what is wrong.

"Flo! Beefheart!" I said, still banging the buttons, but Ramona must have opened the doors above to keep the elevators from operating. "Malcolm, you have to boost me through the hatch."

"No, I'm not letting you up there."

I yanked an empty meal cart out from its stowage sleeve and positioned it under the hatch. "I'm going up there, Malcolm. I have to. You can help me or not."

He arose from Officer Ned's side and reluctantly steadied the cart as I climbed on top of it. I was encouraged to hear Officer Ned admonish me from the floor. "April, don't you dare," he coughed. "Get back here."

I ignored him for two reasons. One, I had to look after Flo and Beefheart. And two, I knew it would make him mad enough to stay alive so he could tear me a new one later. I pushed open the hatch and saw that people were up in the aisles all willy-nilly. *Oh well*, I thought, *it's chaos*, and I flipped open the hatch and popped myself into the aisle, closing it behind me.

Only a few passengers noticed me emerge, and they stared at me in stunned silence. The blood on my white blouse did not help, I thought. But no time to worry about that. I looked around the cabin to assess its condition. The first thing I noticed was Old Cinderblock, or, more accurately, the *absence* of Old Cinderblock. He was not in his seat and was nowhere to be seen. The second thing I noticed was Flo near the aft cross-aisle. She met my eyes and held up her hand in a way that appeared to be meant to warn me away.

I ignored that and ran down the aisle toward her, knocking over two teenagers and that sloppy drunk who had earlier made a scene during boarding. When I reached Flo I saw what she meant when she had tried to warn me away. Lying behind her in the cross-aisle was the air marshal, his lurid Hawaiian shirt practically glowing like plutonium, his Dockers pant leg pushed up to expose an empty holster, a bullet hole in his head that was made, presumably, by his own gun.

"Kid," Flo said sadly, "I tried to tell you to stay back."

It was then that I noticed Ramona, pointing the air marshal's gun at Flo's head.

Lord Christ, I thought to myself, channeling Flo, *how many damn guns are there on this aircraft?* And then, once again, I sprang into action.

In the flight attendant self-defense course, they teach you ways to disarm an assailant, and one of the most interesting things in that training video—to me, anyway—is when the instructor says that he would rather face a gun instead of a knife any day of the week.

"With a gun," he says, "all you have to worry about is the little hole at the end of the barrel. Just make sure that little hole isn't pointing at you and you have a chance of escaping the situation."

One of the interesting things about human anatomy, I learned from this training, is that the wrist is one of the weakest parts of the body. So weak, in fact, that when you smack the back of someone's hand sharply, it easily jackknifes at the wrist and tends to release their grip. "Swat it!" the instructor instructed. "Swat it to the ground!"

So that's exactly what I did. *Swat!* I swatted Ramona's weapon right to the ground. Among the three of us—me, Ramona, and Flo—I think I was probably the most surprised that it actually worked.

When the gun clattered to the floor, I dove for it, along with Ramona and Flo both.

"Flo!" I cried as I struggled with Ramona over the dead body of the air marshal to try and keep her from retrieving his weapon. "Flo, go back to the galley!" She stood, but beyond that did not seem to move. Ramona tried scratching me like a bobcat, but at that precise moment I discovered something new about myself, and that was this: You don't get trapped in a car trunk next to the corpse of one of your only friends, only to escape to find yourself locked up in a hospital about to be turned over to a murderer, only to escape to find yourself on a flight where the three remaining friends you have on this earth—as well as an innocent emotional support dog—are about to be bombed off the planet without growing some steel-clad cojones of your own.

I grabbed the Halon fire extinguisher from its bracket by the cross-aisle jumpseat, snapped the seal, and blasted it in Ramona's face. She screamed and retreated, coughing and spitting and trying to dig the chemical foam from her eye sockets. I had time to feel satisfied for about half a second before I heard a menacing voice from behind me.

"Yoo-hoo," it said.

I turned to see the sloppy drunk grinning at me. Only he didn't seem drunk at all. In fact, he seemed immensely lucid right then—evil, even—seeing as how he was pointing the air marshal's gun at Flo's head.

Dang! I thought. *Did I fall for the oldest trick in the book, or what?* He was the sleeper hijacker. They teach you about this in flight attendant training: Never assume the hijackers who reveal themselves are the only terrorists on the plane.

"Oh, my *God,* just *look* at me!" Ramona griped from behind me. "Jack, can you finish these two, please? I have to try and salvage all this." And she stormed back to the front of the plane past both panicked and oblivious passengers, some of whom still tried to intercept her to ask for beverages. She smacked their hands away and continued storming up the aisle.

"My pleasure," the fake drunk called after her. He said it like it was anything but pleasurable. Then he pushed Flo aside and aimed the gun at me.

Here's the thing about the D zone cross-aisle of an L-1011 aircraft: There's an alcove that runs the length of the cross-aisle. Half of it is a coat closet, and the other half houses a remote raft. They call it "remote" because inflatable rafts are usually located in the slide bustles at each exit door. But this one, this raft at the D zone cross-aisle, is not. It's in the closet, and the inflation handle is easy to find if you're a third-generation flight attendant (although a fake one for now). So I yanked that inflation handle, and the result was as calamitous as you'd expect in an enclosed area where the inflation of a raft the size of a house had just been deployed.

Boom! went the raft as the CO_2 canisters exploded air into its chambers.

Bang! went the air as it popped out of the rubberized canvas when the confines of the cabin proved too tight for the giant raft to expand further.

Aaaaah!! went the screams of the passengers as it finally began to dawn on those in D zone that something was seriously amiss.

When the calamity halfway cleared, I was already up at the mid galley, already inside the elevator, and already descending when I caught sight of Old Cinderblock. He was out of his handcuffs (seriously, there are *hundreds* of videos on YouTube) and he had a yelping Beefheart by the scruff of the neck as he clomped down the aisle on his big Frankenstein feet toward the first-class cabin. I stopped the elevator car and reversed the toggle switches to re-ascend. Then I threw open the door and ran down the aisle after him.

"Grab that dog!" I implored to the passengers nearby. They all screamed in complete and utter uselessness, except for one person on an aisle seat three rows from the first-class curtain. It was a lady who must have been ninety years old with little tiny arms no bigger than broomsticks. She grabbed her cane from underneath the seat in front of her and whacked Old Cinderblock across the hand like an angry Catholic nun. Cinderblock squawked in pain and released his grip on Beefheart, who hit the ground running toward me and jumped in my arms.

I gathered him gratefully and headed back to the mid galley to descend the elevator. Thankfully the fake drunk was still trying to untangle himself from the big, air-blown boa constrictor of the remote raft and had yet to resume his murderous pursuit. Old Cinderblock must have had more pressing things to deal with, because he didn't pursue me, either. I entered the elevator and descended, and was overcome with relief to see that Flo had made it there before me.

I burst through the door of the lift and handed Malcolm the dog. He gathered Beefheart in his arms and pressed his face against the wiry fur of the sweet little beast. "Thank you."

I disabled the lifts by cracking open each door, as the lifts won't function unless the doors on each end are shut securely. I had to close off access. I didn't know what other killers with deceptively friendly faces would come flooding in. Luckily, the hatch could only be opened from below.

We barely had time to take a breath before the intercom blared. "Oh, Flo," Ramona's voice oozed saccharine, "I have somebody here who wants to talk to you."

Ash's nervous voice boomed through the speakers. "Flo, it's Ash Manning. Been a long time, huh? Yeah . . . uh, listen, heh heh, funny thing, there's a guy here with a gun on me, he says he's gonna shoot unless you come up from down there."

Flo began walking toward the lift. I grabbed her arm and pleaded, "No! Are you nuts? *That's Ash!* Don't go, Flo, *please!*"

Even now as I say this, I don't know why Flo didn't just let them shoot Ash. That gun was pretty small caliber. It probably would not have killed him. Besides, her days of caring about passengers were supposed to have been long gone. When I helped her study to take her annual qualifications last year, at the part about how to protect passengers in a hijacking, she laughed, "Use them as a human shield."

But underneath all the cigarettes, the Bloody Marys, the rebellion, and the cragginess, she was still a flight attendant. She had seen it all, survived, and come out stronger on the other side. So maybe way down under that giant hair bun there was something similar to my real father, who, instead of stepping off the plane to save himself, stepped further inside to try to save others. One step is all it takes.

Excuse me . . . sometimes when I talk about my real dad, for some reason out of the blue I might start crying, and I sincerely hate it when that happens. Crying is of no use to anyone. And Flo was hardly any help, either, because sometimes she'd cry, too. Because not only was she the one who introduced my mother to my father, but she also introduced my mother to my stepfather as well.

"So there you go, kid," she'd say, waving the chain-smoke from the galley area. "I am responsible for both the best thing and the worst thing that ever happened to your mother."

Today I tried to keep my grip on Flo's arm, dig in my heels, and force her to stay with me in the tentative safety of the lower galley. But she was strong for a five-feet-nothing, ninety-five-pound firecracker. I couldn't keep her there, or convince her to stay.

"No matter what we think of him," Flo said, "he doesn't deserve to die at the hands of those animals."

"Oh, Flo," I cried. "We see that differently."

Malcolm put his arm around my shoulders, and Flo ascended the lift. We could see her through the window of the lift door as she disappeared to the upper galley. I could hear the lift door above us open and slam against the PA panel, and the scuffling of footsteps. Then the intercom buzzed to life again, and I heard Ramona's slightly Southern-accented voice, twice as menacing now in its treacly friendliness.

"April, sweetheart," she trilled. "You and your friends are gonna have to come up from below. C'mon now."

I settled my roiling fear and anger as best I could, and spoke into the speaker. "Ramona, sweetheart, I would rather drive a railroad spike through my eye."

"I was afraid you'd be that way, darlin', so I hate to say we need to take drastic measures. I have your friend Flo here—" Her words made my face burn. "—and my friend Jack here has a gun to her head. I'm gonna count to twenty, and you and your friends—including the dog, now, don't forget him—better come up from down there and stop fussin' with us, or it just breaks my heart to say that your friendship with Flo here is gonna come to an end real quick."

I said nothing. My hands balled into fists. Ramona knew I wouldn't lift a finger to save Ash Manning, so she got Flo up there to use as leverage instead. I looked at Malcolm frantically, and his expression reflected mine. Officer Ned lay still with his eyes closed, and I wasn't sure he was even conscious.

"I'm gonna start countin' now," Ramona sing-songed. "One . . . two . . . three . . . four . . . five . . . six . . . seven . . . eight . . . nine . . . ten . . . eleven . . . Okay, hey, how 'bout I let Flo have a chance to beg for her life? C'mon on over here, Flo. Here, tell April how Jack's got a gun to your head. Go on, tell her."

I heard Flo's raspy cough, then she said, "Yep, kid. There's a gun to my head, *again*." I began to turn in circles, looking for something, anything, I could think of to use to help gain control of the situation.

"Tell her he's got the barrel cocked," Ramona urged.

"Yep, he's got the barrel cocked."

"Now beg for your life, Flo. C'mon, do it."

Malcolm and I stood frozen in fear and dread. Flo coughed once more, then her voice—her dear, cigarette-shredded voice— came through strong and clear. "April, just remember Mac season two, episode five, and whatever you do, *don't come up here! Don't you dare come—* "

BANG! The sound of the gunshot was so loud through the speaker that I grabbed my head as though I'd been shot myself. *"No!"* I screamed. *"Flo, no! Flo!"*

The speaker was silent but for the cries of the nearby passengers. Then I heard—and I swear I felt it, too—the small thud of Flo's body as it crumpled to the galley floor above my head. I crumpled to the floor myself, too stunned to even cry. Someone was crying, though, softly. I turned to see both Malcolm and Officer Ned weeping into the palms of their hands.

CHAPTER 12

After the screams of the passengers died down, the aircraft fell eerily quiet, and not only did Ramona and the fake drunk stop making demands, but I didn't hear any hijackers trying to bust their way through the hatch to force their way down. They must have thought they were able to regroup and plan their next move. They must have thought we didn't have anywhere to go.

And normally, they would have been right.

I felt Malcolm's hand on my shoulder. "What did she mean by 'Mac, season two, episode . . . .'"

"Episode five," I said softly.

"What was that about?"

I didn't answer him. I wiped away the wetness on my cheeks (I must have cried after all) and forced myself to address the task at hand. "Does your cell phone work up here?" I asked Malcolm.

"No, believe me, I tried," he said, doing his best to stiffen his upper lip.

Many people think cell phone use isn't possible from an aircraft at cruising altitude. They're only half right. Some work, most don't. It's just a matter of seeing which ones do. I remembered the imposter Brighton McPherson's phone, which thankfully Officer Ned had tucked back into the pocket of Beefheart's vest. I grabbed it, dialed 911 and got an operator somewhere in Arkansas.

"I'm on WorldAir flight 1021 and we're being hijacked!" I screamed into the phone.

"What's your name?" the operator asked me.

"April Mae Manning."

"What's the address of the emergency?"

"I just told you. I'm on an aircraft! We're being hijacked! They've killed three people!"

"I can't dispatch the police unless you give me an address," she said curtly. I hung up.

Next I dialed the WorldAir reservation desk, only to be sent to some computer-automated echo chamber. "Representative!" I yelled into the phone. "Representative! . . . Representa . . . *dang it*!" I hung up. "Malcolm, who should I call?"

"Who knows phone numbers? I just click a name on the contact list."

Then Officer Ned—thank God he wasn't dead—reached up and weakly motioned for me to give him the phone. I handed it to him.

"I swear to God, you kids, you don't know any phone numbers?" He winced as he punched in a number. The painkillers were starting to work, I could tell.

"Who are you calling?" I asked.

"The Georgia Bureau of Investigation," he said. Someone must have answered, because he raised his finger to silence me. "Representative!" he croaked into the phone. "Representative! . . . Representa . . . *oh, forget it*!" He hung up, handed the phone back to me, and rested his head back onto the bundle of blankets I'd made him for a pillow.

No time to be frustrated. I dialed 800-444-4444, the number of the old MCI telecommunications technical support line. It was a number so simple it defied forgetfulness. An automated operator answered with, "Welcome to MCI. Our system indicates you are calling from 404-828-8805. If this is the number you are calling about, press one." I hung up.

"Malcolm, write this down: 4-0-4-8-2-8-8-8-0-5," I directed, "it's the number for this phone." Then I dashed over to the pile of useful items collected from the crew bags, grabbed the curling iron and banged it against the counter until the half that was the metal tube broke off. I yanked the heating coil out of it and popped the plastic cap off the top, which left me with a hollow metal tube. Then I opened the packet of spaghetti and inserted a handful of the dry pasta sticks into the tube.

"Can you hand me that PO2 bottle, Malcolm?"

"What is a PO2 bottle?"

"Sorry, it's the oxygen bottle in the bracket to the left of the jumpseat, the one with the rubber yellow mask."

He handed it to me. I tore the rubber mask from the plastic tubing, then inserted the open end of the tubing into one end of the metal pipe filled with spaghetti. I sealed the connection with the masking tape.

"What is that?" Malcolm asked.

"It's a makeshift lance," I said.

"Are you serious? Like the kind bank robbers use to bust open safes?" Of course Malcolm knew what a thermic lance was. "Is it gonna work?"

"I hope so. I learned about it on Gizmodo.com. 'Seven Deadly Weapons You Should Never Ever Make Out of Harmless Household Items.' My grandfather and I did this once, but this is my first time trying it with an authentic pressurized oxygen tank," I said. "The dry spaghetti is supposed to serve as a decent facsimile for conductive aluminum rods."

"*So* awesome."

The walls on an aircraft that separate its compartments are made of material that, though strong, is also as thin and light-weight as possible. It's the perfect material to be strong enough to hold aloft untold tons of cargo, resist impact from blunt blows, and hold up during catastrophic weather conditions. It is *not* ideal to withstand a blowtorch—or, in this case, a thermic lance, which can kind of be described as a blowtorch, but with laser-like precision.

Malcolm gingerly picked up the bag containing the now-dormant explosive device and placed it on the crew stowage shelf, securing it behind the rubber netting. He and I both donned sunglasses we'd collected from the crew bags, and I put on a pair of oven mitts from a drawer next to the reach-in freezer. Then I carried my contraption as far forward in the gal-ley as I could, aimed it at the wall separating us from the cargo bay, pulled Flo's cigarette lighter from my pocket, and held it at the tip of the improvised lance.

"Ready?" asked Malcolm.

"Ready."

"Ready for what?" Officer Ned wailed weakly. "What are you kids doing? Put that thing—"

Malcolm cranked the handle on the tank, which caused the pure oxygen to be released into the metal tube. I waited a few sec-onds to be sure the oxygen had saturated the interior of the metal tube. Then I flicked Flo's lighter to life and touched the flame to the tip of the lance.

"Wow!" Malcolm exclaimed. Even Officer Ned looked a little impressed. The improvised thermic lance beamed like a bionic light saber. I touched the beam to the forward wall and began to burn a circle to open a hole big enough for every one of us to fit through, including Officer Ned. "Malcolm, can you please put the rest of the useful items in my backpack and carry it over here?"

I would have thought there'd have been more sparks, but there weren't, perhaps because the metal material I was torching through wasn't completely solid, but had a corrugated center. There was smoke, though, which set off the alarm positioned over the sink. The beeping could hardly be heard over the sound of the engines, but I told Malcolm to silence it anyway. When the tank ran out of oxygen, I'd finished burning about four-fifths of the circle, creating a large C-shaped cut in the wall. Malcolm turned the crank of the oxygen tank to the off position, and motioned me aside. Then he kicked the center of the C until it bent outward, perching suspended on its remaining hinge like the lid of a can of spinach in the old *Popeye* cartoons.

We stood peering through the opening. It revealed a metal catwalk bordered by cargo areas on each side. At the head of the catwalk was a metal shelving grid that housed a collection of blinking electrical boxes, circuits, and panels.

"What is that?" Malcolm asked.

"That," I said, "is the aircraft avionics area."

PART IX

HOW TO THROW A DEAD BODY OFF AN AIRCRAFT

The word "avionics" is a contraction of the phrase "aircraft electronics," and represents the area of an aircraft that houses the important circuits that manage the aircraft communication system, navigation system, anti-collision system, and multiple other systems. Normally you can find the avionics panel in the cockpit of the aircraft, but with giant, sophisticated jets like the L-1011, the avionics are too large to fit into the cockpit, so they are located in a section of the cargo bay directly below the cockpit. If needed, an L-1011 pilot can access the avionics through a hatch in the floor without having to open the cockpit door.

Malcolm and I walked to the end of the catwalk and studied the cluster of panels closely. I was trying to match it to the memories of the times I helped my airplane-engineer grandfather study for his annual recurrent training. I found the breaker I was looking for and pulled it out.

"What did you just do?" asked Officer Ned, who had emerged directly behind me. He was still missing one boot and hunched over with his arm around the Malcolm's shoulders, who was doing his best to help support him. Beefheart was sitting on his haunches obediently at their feet, his tail stub wagging.

"I think I just dropped all the oxygen masks in the passenger cabins," I said. Above us we could hear a wave of muffled hollering coming from the passengers. So I knew I'd done something.

"What do you mean you *think you dropped the oxygen masks?*" Officer Ned asked.

"Well, I'll know in a second," I said. "If the plane is on autopilot like I suspect, this will make the computer think there's a decompression occurring."

"What does that accomplish?"

Just then we felt the plane begin a sharp dive. The panic of the passengers above us reached a new decibel, then quickly dimmed to an eerie silence. Malcolm and Officer Ned braced themselves against one of the cargo shelves.

"What's happening?" Officer Ned asked, panicked himself.

"When a decompression occurs on an aircraft, the vessel must immediately dive to an altitude below fourteen thousand feet," Malcolm informed him, "which is an altitude that has oxygen dense enough for us to breathe without the need for compressed air."

"Quick, Malcolm, come with me. Officer Ned, you stay here with Beefheart, please." The plane suddenly leveled out, but I knew we only had a few minutes until the autopilot corrected itself and began to climb again.

The PA system crackled to life with Ramona's voice. "Listen, passengers, you better stay seated with your—" she began, but then I reached back and yanked two more breakers from the avionics board. Sparks leapt from the panel.

"What was that?" Malcolm asked as he followed me back into the galley.

"I just blew the plane's PA and interphone system," I said.

"You pulled *two* breakers just now."

"Yeah, I also shorted out all cockpit communication."

"Wow." Malcolm whistled under his breath.

We crawled back through the opening to the lower galley. I yanked the meal cart containing the body of the imposter Brighton McPherson out of the stowage sleeve ("It's all in the leverage") and rolled it near the small access door in the fuselage that the catering crew uses at the gate when they board supplies. The plane had just dipped below fourteen thousand feet; the cabin pressure automatically adjusted accordingly, I surmised, so this door should open.

The imposter's body was positioned in the meal cart so that when you opened the front flap all you saw was his back, where a tattoo of three tiny black birds trailed from the base of his neck into his collar. I uncapped the Sharpie marker and, across the back of his white regulation work shirt, I wrote, "WorldAir flight

1021. We are being hijacked. Please don't shoot us down! Call 404-828-8805." Then I opened the exterior door.

The rush of air was deafening, but since we were at an altitude of sustainable density, not much got sucked through the opening except some loose debris and a crew bag or two. Once opened, the door raised itself on tracks and stayed flush with the curve of the ceiling. Malcolm and I each held a handgrip on either side of the door frame with one hand, then reached back with the other to grasp the pull bar of the meal cart to draw it forward. I hadn't meant to discard the cart along with the body, but once the momentum got started it was hard not to. The cart and body both tumbled out of the aircraft and separated in midair. The imposter Brighton McPherson somersaulted in one direction, while the cart went in the other.

I froze for a second, praying no one would get hurt on the ground. The plane began to climb. Some more debris started to sweep out of the door, so Malcolm and I reached for the buttress grips at the foot of the door and began pulling down mightily to try to close it.

Officer Ned stood unsteadily peering at us through the hole I'd created in the galley wall. Among the unsecured, lighter-weight items that were being blown across the galley floor and out the door was his black motorcycle boot.

"The boot!" he squawked. "Get the boot!"

Unfortunately Beefheart, highly trained and dedicated as he was, took this as an extension of his earlier command. He sprang forward from behind Officer Ned, ran across the galley, leapt through the air, sunk his teeth into the boot . . . *and got sucked right out the door with it!*

"*Beefheart!*" Malcolm and I screamed in unison.

Then I screamed even louder. I didn't think I could scream so loud. In fact, I screamed so loud I'm pretty sure that not only the people in the cabin above heard me, but also people here on the ground. Because Malcolm—and this is still really hard for me to say—okay, Malcolm . . . wait, I need to take a sip of Gatorade . . . Malcolm, you see, without even a scintilla of hesitation, Malcolm *let go of the door and dove out of the plane after Beefheart.*

It seriously seemed like the world stopped right then. Like, I remember once when I took a trip with my mother to an old gold-mining town in north Georgia called Dahlonega, and right there in the town square was a general store that sold moccasins and slingshots and penny candy and all kinds of other old-fashioned things, but the best part was that they had a whole row of those old-timey Nickelodeon viewers that show movies by flipping pictures on a giant Rolodex. I remember I could view the movie as fast or as slow as I wanted, and it always took me forever to complete the show, because I would stop each picture and examine it like a slide under a microscope.

That's what it was like in this case, when all the friends I had left in the world, all three, dove out of the airplane. It was like that Nickelodeon viewer—really, really, super slow. The scenes went by like flip . . . stop . . . flip . . . stop . . . flip . . . stop.

Flip, there goes Captain Beefheart out the door after Officer Ned's motorcycle boot.

Flip, there goes Malcolm out the door after Captain Beefheart.

Flip, *there goes Officer Ned out the door after Malcolm!*

And then everything sped up again.

Flipflipflipflipflipflip!

Even with two bullets and three painkillers in him, it's astounding how fast that Officer Ned could move. He shot out the door like a rocket and grabbed Malcolm by the waistband of his jeans, just as he was about to go sailing into the wild blue yonder. I could hear both of them bang against the exterior of the plane.

As I said, the catering portal is not like a regular passenger door. It's smaller and narrower, and Officer Ned had splayed his legs open so his bottom half stayed wedged inside the plane. I reached out and grabbed Officer Ned by his belt and tried to pull with all my might.

Flipflipflipflipflipflip!

Somehow, I don't know how, Officer Ned was able to reach back and grab the assist handle along the interior frame of the portal—maybe he had hold of it all along, I don't know, but it certainly seemed like he was free-flying there at first. It certainly seemed like I was about to lose everybody, there, and if that had happened I seriously don't know if I might have lost all hope and simply stepped out after them. One wrong step is all it takes, remember? Out instead of in. Forward instead of back. I really think I might have just stepped out after them.

But Officer Ned got hold of that assist handle and was able to pull Malcolm back inside, along with himself. All three of us fell onto the mat. I immediately clambered back up to grab the door handle and try to pull it shut. The plane was climbing, though. The air in the fuselage was compressing, creating a dense force that pushed outward on the walls of the aircraft. I wasn't strong enough, and the longer it took to close the door the harder it would be to close at all, and if we didn't close the door soon then the altitude would thin out the oxygen, we'd pass out and every last thing in that galley that wasn't bolted down would get sucked from the fuselage. Including us. We were far from bolted down.

I struggled with the door until I thought I'd break in half, then suddenly Officer Ned's arms appeared in my peripheral vision and grasped the door lever above me. With a mighty tug we were able to close the door and lock the lever. The engines still roared loudly as always, but it seemed quiet as a meadow now in comparison to having the exterior door open during flight. I turned to Officer Ned, so grateful I wanted to throw my arms around him. But when I caught sight of his face I stopped.

"Are you . . . ." he began, his face as gray as asphalt. Then his eyes rolled back in their sockets and he hit the ground like a safe. I stood there, a little stunned by the events that had just transpired.

"Oh, man," I heard Malcolm groan, still gasping for breath, "it's like I have the world's worst wedgie right now."

It wasn't until then that I noticed—clutched tightly in Malcolm's arms—dear Captain Beefheart, his sweet, incongruously feminine eye-linered eyes bright with excitement, his tail stub wiggling. Officer Ned's boot was still grasped in his teeth. I thought it was the most beautiful thing I'd ever seen. I collapsed to the ground myself, ready to crack up laughing. I had the smile on my face and everything. But the funny thing is I burst into sobs instead.

PART X

THE COCKPIT BREACH

FBI Telephone Conversation Transcript, cont.
404-828-8805
04/01/2013, 12:22 P.M.

Agent Kowalski:
Young lady, tell me exactly who you are and what is going on up there. Immediately. And where did you get this phone?

April Manning:
I'm in the cargo hold. I got this phone from the pocket of someone who was trying to murder my friend. I tried calling the FBI directly, but your receptionist is really picky about who she puts through. I think you need a new training program.

Agent Kowalski:
Who are you?

April Manning:
I'm an unaccompanied minor on board WorldAir flight 1021. I don't have a lot of time. The plane is being hijacked. Let me tell you what I need—

Agent Kowalski:
Are you making demands?

April Manning:
I guess it depends on how you look at it. I just need you to please not shoot us down just yet.

Agent Kowalski:
It's not up to me. It's up to the president, the NTSB, and the FAA. Has the cockpit been breached?

April Manning:
I'm pretty sure.

Agent Kowalski:
Unless communication is reestablished with the pilots, I can't say what will happen.

April Manning:
Can you get a message to them?

Agent Kowalski:

Can you tell me what happened to my informant?

April Manning:

Your informant tried to kill a flight attendant on board, but it backfired on him. I mean, like, literally.

Agent Kowalski:

What do you need me to tell the NTSB and the FAA?

April Manning:

Three things:

1. Please give me twenty minutes before you deploy counter measures. I think I can regain control of the cockpit.
2. The old fax machine in the flight deck runs on a different frequency than the cockpit radio. So we can receive faxes, but not send them. Please find the number and fax the coordinates needed for landing this thing. Make sure not to fax it now, but at least twenty minutes from now.
3. There's a bomb on board. I'm sending you a picture of it right now.

CHAPTER 13

We didn't have much time to sit around, relieved and grateful that the four of us hadn't just performed a 'chuteless formation dive out the galley door—but believe me, we were. As soon as I got my bearings I was up again, heading for the opening in the galley wall that led to the plane's avionics, followed by Malcolm, who had fashioned a baby sling out of an airline blanket and now kept Captain Beefheart tied in there, tucked snugly against his chest. Officer Ned, whom we had revived by letting Beefheart lick his face until he opened his eyes, followed us as well. I'd given Officer Ned another painkiller from Flo's supply, and while I was rummaging in her bag I found the three other bullets missing from her gun's chamber.

"Are you sure you're okay?" I asked Officer Ned.

"I'm fine," he said, sounding anything but. "This is not my first time."

"Not your first time doing what?" Malcolm asked.

"Not my first time getting shot."

Officer Ned gulped down the painkiller gratefully without even needing any water, while Malcolm and I glanced at each other in mutual admiration of him. The wound on his arm had started bleeding again, probably due to the exertion from the incident at the galley door, while the wound at his rib seemed bearable for him if he clutched it tightly while he limped.

"At least I have both my boots now," he said. I thought he was going for levity, but if so his expression sure hadn't gotten the message.

I had one foot through the opening in the bulkhead when suddenly the lights went out. *Blink.* I mean all of them. It was pitch-black down there but for a tiny ray of daylight coming through a small porthole in the galley door, which did us no good.

"What's going on?" Officer Ned whispered.

"Someone at the flight attendant control panel must have knocked out all the lights," I answered. Since there weren't any menacing attempts to get at us from above, I suspected the hijackers assumed we weren't much of a threat. They probably thought Officer Ned was dead or close to it, and Malcolm and I were just unaccompanied minors. What did we know.

"What do we do?" Malcolm asked.

I rifled through my bag and produced the carabiner with the pin light, the one I'd used weeks ago in Cinderblock's trunk. "Take this," I said, and handed it to Officer Ned. It didn't do much in terms of illumination, but at least it was something. "There should be a flashlight under the jumpseat. I can feel my way back there. I'll be right back. Both of you stay here."

They ignored me without hesitation and followed me back into the galley.

Each aircraft jumpseat is equipped with a regulation flashlight nearby to be used in the event of an emergency, and in the case of the L-1011 it is secured by a Velcro strap beneath the fold-down seat. But when I felt for it, it wasn't there. It must have been knocked loose during all the ruckus and had likely been blown out with the other unsecured items when the galley door was open. *Dang!* I thought. Then Malcolm spoke up.

"Did I see some baking soda in the refrigerator earlier?" he asked.

I nodded, then remembered he couldn't see me. "Yes, why?" I asked.

"Where is it?" he asked. I could hear his hands patting the stowage flaps, looking for the one that led to the refrigerator.

"It's the last flap on your left. Just flip up the toggles over the handle to unlock it."

He did so, and asked Officer Ned to shine the pin light inside. "Aha!" he said. "April, can you bring me a plastic water bottle from the beverage cart . . . no, not that one, the big one . . . and a couple of cans of Mountain Dew? Great, thanks. And where is the first aid kit?"

"What are you doing?" Officer Ned asked. I had an idea of the answer, and was excited to see if it would work.

"Just watch," Malcolm said.

He unscrewed the water bottle and poured its contents down the sink. Then he opened the cans of Mountain Dew and, as best he could in the dim light, he transferred the beverage into the plastic bottle.

"What do you need from the first aid kit?" I asked.

"A couple of sterile wipes," he responded.

I unwrapped the wipes from their packets and handed them to him. He wadded them up and dropped them into the bottle. They splashed quietly into the Mountain Dew. Malcolm then knocked about a teaspoon of the baking soda into the palm of his hand and gently brushed that into the mixture as well. Lastly, he recapped the bottle and shook it vigorously.

The result was splendiferous. The liquid inside glowed a bright, luminescent green, brighter than a traffic signal. It was so bright it lit the galley enough for me to read a newspaper if I wanted.

I clapped my hands in excitement. "So *totally* awesome!"

"What *is* that?" Officer Ned asked.

"You haven't seen the video? It's a YouTube sensation," Malcolm explained. "You just mix Mountain Dew with a bit of baking soda, add a little hydrogen peroxide . . . ."

"The sterile wipes!" I said.

" . . . right, the sterile wipes that come in first aid kits usually contain hydrogen peroxide, or at least I was banking on the fact that these did."

Officer Ned looked impressed. "How does *that* happen?" He pointed to the bottle of glowing liquid.

"It's just a chemical reaction that causes the liquid to glow like plutonium," Malcolm answered, adding, "for some reason."

I wanted to kiss him, but I didn't know how long the light would last inside the bottle. So I simply swore I'd never drink Mountain Dew again (I bet chemical toilets are composed of more organic ingredients), and the three of us ventured back through the hole in the wall and into the cargo bay.

One thing I'd noticed when Malcolm was retrieving the baking soda was that the cooler door, when open, lay flat against the bulkhead and concealed the top half of the hole I'd created. So once we were through, I opened the cooler door behind us and pulled out a heavy beverage cart from the nearest sleeve and secured its brake, which in turn concealed the lower half of the hole. It wasn't a David Copperfield illusion, but I thought it would work to cover our tracks for a bit, especially in a pitch-dark galley.

As we crept along the catwalk, Malcolm asked me, "What did Flo mean by that message she told you through the intercom?"

I stopped for a moment as the thought of Flo sent a wave of despondence through my entire body. It was literally a physical effort to push it aside in order to forge ahead. *I can't fall apart about Flo right now,* I thought. I'd fall apart about her tomorrow, and the day after, and so on. But right now was not the time.

"It's an episode of *MacGyver*. Other than that, I'm not sure what she meant," I admitted.

"You don't know the episode she's talking about?" he asked. "Let's get out your DVDs and read the episode summaries."

"Actually, I know the episode she was referring to really well; I just don't know how she meant for it to help us in this situation."

"Well, little lady." Officer Ned's speech was beginning to slur a little due to the painkillers, and I could see through the glow of Malcolm's Mountain Dew lantern that he grinned dreamily. "Why don't you go on and tell us what the episode is about, and maybe we can put our heads together and come up with some suggestions."

"Okay," I agreed. "In this episode, MacGyver takes a trip to the wilderness with a bunch of gang-member delinquents as part of some probation program—"

"What wilderness, where?" Officer Ned asked thoughtfully. He furrowed his brow and stroked his goatee like Sigmund Freud.

"It's in the mountains somewhere, at a high altitude. He travels there in a plane—"

"A plane!" Officer Ned exclaimed, like it was a big breakthrough.

"Yes, a plane. It's a small Cessna aircraft. He and the kids are flown there by a pilot who has a heart attack and dies on the way back from picking them up—"

"Heart attack!" Another breakthrough for Officer Ned.

"Yes, the pilot dies mid-flight. Mac has to land the plane in the mountains and they all end up stranded."

"Hmmm. What else?"

"Um . . . I don't think there's any more important information from the episode."

"Young lady." Officer Ned attempted to puff out his chest and sound authoritative, but the bullet wounds and the painkillers prevented that. "I am an officer of the *law*," he continued as best he could. "I am an expert in *detection*. I am trained to look at the most minuscule of details and develop a *theory*! Now, what else happens in the episode?"

"Uh, okay," I said, and continued to describe the details of the episode, about how the delinquents were a group of four—three guys and one girl—and how they all came from rival gangs, how one got saved from a rattlesnake when Mac used a smoldering piece of wood from the fire to create warmth to attract the snake away from the sleeping bag, and how another got saved from a mountain lion when Mac used a hollow log to divert water to splash on it because everyone knows cats hate water, and how Mac tried to dissipate the infighting of the delinquents by assigning them tasks to create camaraderie, and how, in the end, he was able to repair the damaged aircraft and fly them all to safety.

Officer Ned and Malcolm began to theorize amongst themselves. Soon they were dissecting every detail and even delving into the subliminal side of things.

"A group of four delinquents, I bet that signifies the four cabins on the L-1011 plane," Malcolm began.

"Oooh, good one," Officer Ned interjected, "and the mountain lion must represent the flight attendant who shot me, and the rattlesnake represents the man who shot Flo . . . ."

"I hadn't thought of that! Of course they do!"

"And the tension between MacGyver and the group of kids represents the struggle between innovation and authority . . . ."

"Uh . . . oh-kay."

"Like, how you could be turned down for promotion four times even though you took two bullets for your partner, who got his promotion, didn't he? Yes he did, but me? No, not me. All I got was stuck doing these prisoner escort assignments, and why? Because I don't bow to The Man, that's why . . . ."

"Officer Ned, let's bring it back to the message in the *Mac-Gyver* episode," Malcolm urged patiently. I had a feeling Malcolm was experienced in bringing people back from the precipice of a prescription drug–induced rant. Remember, I'd met his mother.

"Right, yes." Officer Ned immediately returned to the task at hand. "Uh, okay, there's four kids, maybe that's the number of hijackers we're dealing with . . . ." His previous rambling did make me remember something, though. It was an incident early in the episode in which MacGyver plucks a canister of pills from the dead pilot's breast pocket and murmurs to himself, "Nitroglycerin."

Nitroglycerine is famous for two things. One, it's super highly explosive; in fact it's the ingredient that make dynamite sticks go boom. And two, nitroglycerin, taken in minuscule amounts, can be used as a medicine that opens blood vessels to improve blood flow in order to allay a heart attack, or simply to alleviate chest pains during angina. Plenty of passengers experience chest pains on long flights—in fact, I'm sure there were plenty above us right then, clutching their chests and being ignored by the imposter-laden cabin crew—which is why WorldAir always keeps a canister containing twenty-five tablets of nitroglycerin on every aircraft located in the emergency medical kit!

"Malcolm," I said, interrupting his and Officer Ned's florid attempts to decipher the symbolism of every scene in the *MacGyver* episode. ("The plane, you see, represents our soaring dreams, only to come crashing to the ground.") "Malcolm, can you hand me the EMK?"

"What's an EMK?" he asked.

"Emergency medical kit," I clarified. "You brought it with you, right?"

"You bet I did." He handed it to me.

I plunked it at my feet and crouched down to rummage through the transparent pockets on the inside sleeves where all the medications reserved for physicians' use were stowed. Malcolm situated his Mountain Dew lantern to aid me.

"Found it!" I exclaimed, brandishing the canister.

"What is that?" Malcolm asked. Officer Ned was beginning to look worried again.

"Nitroglycerin tablets."

"So totally awesome! Are you gonna use them to blow your way through the cockpit?"

Officer Ned stepped between me and Malcolm. "Wait, hold on now, just what are you planning to do?"

"We need to blow through the hatch in the floor of the flight deck in order to gain control of the cockpit—"

"No, not on your life, no." Officer Ned shook his head and actually wagged his finger at me. "You are not using those to blow anything up. Hand them over to me."

I tucked the tablets into the pocket of my apron. Officer Ned was not the only one who could ignore directions. "You didn't let me finish." I was starting to get exasperated. "Of course I'm not gonna use these tablets to blow anything up. These are not explosive, they're medication." Believe me, I knew. Flo had set me straight when I'd griped that MacGyver had neglected to use the tablets to his benefit when we'd watched the episode together.

"Then what were you planning to use to blow into the cockpit?" he asked.

"These," I said, producing the three bullets I'd collected from the bottom of Flo's bag.

"Are you nuts?" Officer Ned asked. "Those are just bullets! You need a gun to use them."

"We see that differently," I told him.

CHAPTER 14

We continued our progress along the catwalk in the cargo bay. I was in front, Malcolm behind me with the lantern in his hand and Captain Beefheart snuggled securely to his chest in the improvised baby sling, and Officer Ned bringing up the rear, limping along with his hand on Malcolm's shoulder. On either side of us were the passengers' checked bags, stacked with all the order and care that big banks might give to the possessions of people evicted from their foreclosed homes.

When I reached the avionics area, I directed the others to follow me as I climbed past the shelves and crawled through to get to the platform on the other side. Malcolm and I made it through easily, even with Beefheart strapped to Malcolm's chest, while Officer Ned ambled up and over with the grace of a wounded water buffalo. True, he was shot up and all, but still, it amounted to a moment of much-needed comic relief for me and Malcolm.

"Stop laughing!" he admonished us. "Seriously, you kids, *this is serious.*"

He was right, of course, but, and I realize I'm speaking for Malcolm here, we really could have used a little levity right then, considering the day's events, which included the dead air marshal, the dead real Brighton McPherson, the dead imposter Brighton McPherson, the almost-dead Malcolm, Beefheart, and Officer Ned, and I don't even want to talk about Flo, and this doesn't even count my dead friend Jalyce Sanders. Yes, this was serious— very, very serious—but such seriousness can weigh on you like a necklace of anvils. Unless you take it off, you can't move because you're so paralyzed. So we laughed.

Because we had to move.

Once Officer Ned had climbed to our side, I had Malcolm raise the lantern to illuminate the ceiling above us. We were looking at the other side of the floor hatch that opened into the cockpit, the one a pilot would use if he wanted to come down and access the avionics area from the flight deck.

This was not a cockpit door. The cockpit door was an opening that led to the passenger cabin. That door had been retrofitted and fortified with enough security measures to keep a cavalcade of elephants from breaking it down. The flight deck floor hatch on an L-1011 exists for the purpose of utility, not as a formal aircraft exit or entrance. It's accessed on the ground when mechanics and engineers need to address any adjustments in order to maintain the operational health of the aircraft. It's accessed during flight when pilots need to address equipment failure. Officially. Flo had regaled me with stories, though, of back in the day when many a pilot and flight attendant, or even pilot and passenger, earned their "mile-high" status by descending through the hatch to engage in amorous activity. Of course, she included herself in that group.

But never in the history of aviation—and I'm not exaggerating here—has the flight deck hatch been breached from beneath during flight. To achieve that would have meant someone had cut a hole through the bulkhead wall beneath, traversed the catwalk through cargo, and climbed past the avionics area to stand where we were, looking up at it from below. So no small feat, right?

Right?

Fine. I just wanted to take a moment to acknowledge the enormity of what we were about to do, since we didn't have time to while we were actually doing it.

Agent Kowalski:

Just finish your statement, please.

April Manning:

Okay, we were looking up at a watertight deck hatch like the kind you'd find on a boat. Back in the fifties and sixties when luxury airliners were being built by Lockheed and Boeing, they used nautical references all the time in their designs, because aircrafts were considered ships in the sky, kind of. That's why you'll hear the cabin crews use terms like "forward" and "aft," and why some airlines refer to the cabin-crew coordinator as "purser." The word "cabin" itself is even a nautical term.

So, again, the floor hatch was literally like a deck hatch on a boat, secured by medium-weight slip-click hardware with a single lock. The hinges were on the opposite side from us, so I couldn't disassemble them, but I could discern from the bolts opposite them where the locking lever was located.

I produced one of the bullets from my pocket and tried to bite the base off of it, but I wasn't doing a good job.

"What are you doing?" Officer Ned whispered.

"I'm trying to bite off the base so I can remove the gunpowder."

Officer Ned thrust out his hand. "Give me one." I passed one to him and continued struggling with my own. In the end, Officer Ned opened both bullets (he had really strong teeth) and I folded the gunpowder from them into a large square bandage from the first aid kit, careful to make sure the sticky edges were sealed together to make a snug little pouch for the powder, which I then crammed into the seam of the hatch directly under the lock. I shoved the remaining bullet in after it and was pleased to see it stuck in there pretty well, with the base protruding out about a quarter of an inch.

"Okay," I whispered to Officer Ned. "Gimme one of your boots."

"What?" He took a small, protective step back. "No! I need these boots!"

"Officer Ned," I addressed him impatiently. "We need something to bang against that bullet. Malcolm is wearing tennis shoes, and I just have on a pair of loafers. The heel of your boot is the hardest thing we have." I refrained from saying "other than your head," because that was just too easy. "So hand it over."

He glared at me sternly, like he was really going to fight me on this, then he deflated and rolled his eyes. "Fine!" He leaned against the metal access ladder and pulled off his left boot. "Take it. Just . . . take it." He handed me the boot. Seriously, what was it about Officer Ned and his boots?

I thanked him, and asked him and Malcolm to stand aside in case there was any, like, shrapnel or something from the fallout of blowing the hatch open. Officer Ned then tried to insist that he be the one to bang the bullet with his own boot, but I talked him out of it for two reasons. One, he already had a bullet in his ribs, which really diminished his ability to swing in an upward thrust. And two, I didn't trust him to really give it a whack, seeing as how he was so attached to that boot and all.

Then Malcolm tried to insist that he be the one to swing the boot, but all I had to do was point to Captain Beefheart all swaddled to his chest like a papoose and say, "Think again, Pocahontas." So they both stood aside and braced themselves while I used Officer Ned's boot to wallop the base of that bullet as hard as I could.

My advice would be to never try this at home. In fact, don't ever try it on an aircraft, either, unless said aircraft happens to be getting hijacked and you really have nothing to lose. Because we were not exactly sneaking up on them with this approach, what with the deafening *Bang! Pow!* that resulted in the explosion, albeit a controlled explosion. Kind of. Because there was a bit of shrapnel, which explains the black stippling on the side of my face right now. And the smoke. I haven't even mentioned the smoke!

We didn't wait for the smoke to clear. Instead, the three of us held our breath and quickly pushed up on the underside of the hatch, expecting some resistance. Surprisingly, there was none. It flew open and the three of us burst through like a trio of coughing, dirty, bleeding jack-in-the-boxes with fists flying.

I was the first to clamber up the ladder and into the cockpit, with Officer Ned following close behind. Again, that man can move fast, even injured and hopped up on OxyContin. He simply sprang up and landed crouched like a cougar at my side, he even somehow had time to put his boot back on. Malcolm made it in about as far as the tops of his shoulders, with little Beefheart's face peeking up curiously from under his chin. All of us were tensed and ready for a fight, just as soon as we finished coughing and waving the smoke from our eyes. In the confusion, I could have sworn I heard a familiar voice. I fruitlessly tried to rub the sting from my eyes and steel myself for the inevitable enemy assault. I flailed my arms madly, but only encountered air and smoke. Then I heard it again. The voice.

"Christ, kid," Flo groused. "What took you so long?"

CHAPTER 15

"Flo!" I yelped. It would have been a scream, but I had a throat full of gunpowder smoke, which tends to constrict your ability in that regard. "Flo!" I threw my arms around her.

"Watch it!" she warned, careful to keep from burning me with the tip of her cigarette like a bad crack mother. Then she realized I was crying and gave into my embrace. "Oh, okay now," she said, the cigarette held at a distance. "There, there. Okay, stop your blubbering. C'mon now. You, too, Thor."

"I'm not crying," he insisted. "The smoke is stinging my eyes."

"Why didn't you just open the hatch from your side to let us in?" Malcolm asked.

"I don't have the key to that thing. Do you see any keys on me?"

"I thought you were dead!" I sobbed. "I thought he shot you!"

"He did, the bastard."

I pulled away to assess her condition. She looked even worse than I did. The customary wedding cake–sized bun on her head looked like it had been detonated by a land mine. Blackened tufts spiked up through the teased white wonderland that was her regular hair color. Then the realization struck me.

"Your bun!" I said. Of course! That bun had been deceiving people into thinking she was an inch and a half taller for forty-six years.

"Yep, saved by the bun." She patted the mess on her head. "It even took a minute for them to realize I wasn't dead."

"And they didn't come back to finish the job?"

"Well, yeah, but somebody intervened."

"Who?"

She took a drag on her cigarette, then she studied the smoke wafting from its tip and said, "Ash."

"Ashtray's right there." I pointed to the ashtray in the armrest of the pilot's jumpseat, a design feature left over from the days when smoking was legal on aircrafts.

"No, April. *Ash.*"

I looked at her in puzzlement. Why did she keep saying "ash?" I was showing her that the ashtray was right . . . .

"Wait, *what*? You mean *Ash*? Ash *Manning*?" I shook my head. "He's the one who got them to get you to come up from the lower galley. Since when does he show a molecule of compassion for anyone? Why would he suddenly grow a backbone?"

"Well, maybe it's because I'm kind of related to him."

"What? How?"

"He's sort of my son."

"What do you mean, *'sort of your son'*?"

"I don't know, kid, the seventies were such a blur. For all I know, Thor here is my son, too."

Officer Ned chuckled at that. It was the closest thing to an actual laugh I'd ever seen come out of him.

"Flo," I implored, "how come you never told me this?"

"He's not exactly something to brag about, kid. We haven't spoken in years. He didn't even intervene on my behalf until after they'd already shot me!"

Huh, she was right about that. I was relieved I could continue to hate him as intensely as always, the spiky old bag of asses that he was. Malcolm cleared his throat to remind me we had important business at hand, and we should readdress it immediately. I looked down at his head sticking up from the floor hatch, and he nodded it sideways to direct my attention to the pilot's seat.

Right! The plane, who was piloting the plane? I turned my head to see Cinderblock at the wheel.

CHAPTER 16

Officer Ned intercepted me before I could attack him.

"Calm down, April," he said.

"That guy tried to kill me!" I hissed. "He killed my friend Jalyce! He's a murdering, mean old kidnapping . . . and he is not a pilot!"

"April, I said calm down," Officer Ned repeated.

Cinderblock turned to face us and rested his elbow on the back of the pilot seat. "I am too a pilot, little miss wildcat," he said. "Or I used to have a private pilot's license, anyway."

"Arrest him!" I demanded of Officer Ned.

"April, this is the third time now I've told you to calm down." He was clutching his side in pain. I ignored him, plunked myself down in the engineer's chair, and began digging through my bag. "What are you doing?"

I found the handcuffs, pulled them out, and headed for Cinderblock. "I'm making a citizen's arrest!"

"Those are my handcuffs! I wondered what happened to them! Hand them back to me right now!"

"All right! *Enough!*" Flo could holler pretty loud for a tiny lady. Plus, in order to clap her hands vigorously to get our attention, she had snuffed out a perfectly good half-finished cigarette. Again, if you knew Flo, that should signal the gravity of the situation. "Hugh," she said to Cinderblock, "tell her."

"I'll tell her," Officer Ned interjected. "April, this is Hugh Newman. He's my former partner."

"Pleased to meet you," Cinderblock said to me.

"I think we've met." I glared at him.

"Let me finish, April," said Officer Ned. "Hugh and I used to be partners in the Atlanta police department, but then I got shot—"

"I see you're still a magnet for bullets, Ned," Cinderblock chuckled.

"—and he got promoted to do undercover work. When you sent me the e-mail about Jalyce Sanders—"

"That was an anonymous e-mail," I said.

"Maybe you thought so, but I could tell it was you. Anyway, when you sent me the e-mail, I knew you were talking about Hugh's investigation. So I gave him a call. We got together and discussed some details—"

"Jalyce Sanders? Is she just a *detail*?" I fumed.

"No," said Cinderblock. "She was an undercover investigator, a really good one, too. God bless her soul."

"I . . . wait, she was?" Wow, this would explain why she knew so much about sociopaths and serial killers. "Then why did you kill her? *Why did you try to kill me?*"

"I didn't kill Maryanne—her real name was Maryanne—I didn't kill her. That was that skinny witch Kathy, she did that. I was just infiltrating their money-laundering ring as a bodyguard—"

"Henchman," Officer Ned interrupted.

"Okay, henchman, and she asked me to help her get rid of Maryanne's body, and it turned into this whole 'oh, by the way, can we swing by and kidnap this little hell-on-wheels wildcat while we're at it and kill her, too' kinda thing."

"So you were gonna kill me to keep from blowing your cover?"

"No, I was gonna stop it before it got that far," he said. Then, under his breath, "Probably."

I paused to think for a second. This solved the puzzle of the second Jalyce Sanders, as presumably she had been replaced with another investigator. Poor Jalyce, or Maryanne. I felt my heart tug. "Wait, what's this about a money-laundering ring?"

"He can't go into detail about that, April. It's still an active investigation," Officer Ned explained.

"Oh, *now* we're keeping secrets," I griped. "Then why were you taking Beefheart to the front cabin?" I asked Cinderblock, referring to the time when the old lady had thwacked him with her cane to allow me to retrieve the dog.

"Beats me," he answered. "I was just doing what I was told. I'm a henchman. That's what I do."

Malcolm finally piped up from his perch on the access ladder just below the hatch. "Flo, what did you mean by 'Mac, season two, episode five?' Was it the mountain lion? And how it represents the hijacker with the gun?"

"And the snake, remember the snake?" asked Officer Ned. "What did the snake represent?"

Flo looked at them like they'd each grown an extra arm out of their foreheads, then turned to me and asked, "Did you bring the nitroglycerin tablets?"

"Yeah." I reached into my pocket and handed them to her. "Why do you need them?"

"Right! Nitro tabs!" Officer Ned exclaimed. "For the heart attack! The pilot had a heart attack, remember?" he nudged Malcolm.

"How did we miss that?" Malcolm said.

Then Officer Ned straightened sharply. "The pilot had a heart attack?"

"Relax, Thor," Flo said. "Nobody had a heart attack—except for maybe one or two of the passengers."

"So you need the nitro tabs for them?"

"Hell, no. They'll be fine. I need the nitro tabs for the hijackers. Right now they've got the pilots hogtied on the floor of the first-class cabin. I have to say it's one of the more satisfying sights I've ever seen, but we've got to bring the fun to an end and get them back in here to land the plane before we get shot out of the sky." She motioned my attention to the cockpit window, where a Navy fighter jet could be seen monitoring us with missiles at the ready.

"Crap!" I said. "Holy crap!" Then suddenly a mechanical whirring sound arose from the flight panel.

"What's that sound?" Cinderblock frantically assessed the flight panel.

The fax machine on the control panel of an L-1011 is not like the kind you see in hotel lobbies and outdated offices. It's a small metal box built into the instruments that blends in with all the other metal doo-jigs in the cockpit. When it jumps to life, it sounds like a lawnmower starting up. Cinderblock couldn't even figure out where the sound was coming from until the thermal mimeograph-type paper began spitting through the little slit in the metal. "What is that?" He pointed to it.

"That should be the coordinates to land the plane," I said, tearing off the paper and studying it.

Flo continued to brief us on her knowledge of the present situation. It went thusly: All together there were four hijackers, Ramona, Kathy, the fake drunk, and that imposter Brighton McPherson that we'd thrown off the plane ("That we know of," I added, determined not to fall for another sleeper). Presently the hijackers had cleared the first-class cabin of passengers and were using it as a command center.

Surprisingly, they had not planned to hijack the plane today. It was a spur-of-the-moment thing. They had planned for this day to go as smoothly as any of the many other days they'd spent smuggling money to and from the liberal banks in the Cayman Islands. "But then they got a message from their boss telling them that you were on the plane, April," Flo said, "and, for some reason, it was necessary to keep you from getting off alive."

"Me? Why?"

"I don't know, kid. But it partly explains why you've been shot at twice today. No other passengers have been shot at."

"I've been shot at," Officer Ned said.

"No, you blocked April while *she* was being shot at," she corrected him.

"You've been shot at," he said.

"I am not a passenger, Thor. I am a crew member, and they only shot at me to try to get to her. April here is the only one who has had two deliberate attempts on her life."

"Three," I corrected. "Let's not forget when I got kidnapped and thrown in a car trunk with a corpse." I glared at Cinderblock.

"Right, three," Flo agreed. "But only twice today." She went on to tell us that the note I'd left on the seat really wrecked the smugglers' plans, too, because if the plane was diverted due to a bomb scare they knew they'd have to disembark without their bags and stand by as the entire airplane got searched by the DEA and all the other formidable government agencies with initials ending in "A" (TSA, FAA, CIA, and probably the NRA, who knows). Their big bag of money would definitely get discovered. So they had to improvise.

"What big bag of money?" I asked. "Malcolm and I went through all the crew bags, there was no money."

"That's just it, I don't think there is a bag of money," she surmised. "I think this time they were given a bag with something else in it."

"The bomb!" Malcolm exclaimed.

"Right, the bomb."

I shook my head. This was too much. I knew Ash was a gutless bovine, but even he wouldn't bring a bomb on a plane, would he? Then I remembered the candy-colored locks on the bag, and it occurred to me that his role was not to look inside. His role was to blindly just bring the bag on the plane and not ask questions.

"Flo, how do you know all this?" Officer Ned asked.

"Ramona and her cronies are not keeping any secrets from us. Alby and I pick up what we can and compare notes. The other flight attendants just sit in first class doing nothing. Granted, they have a gun on them, but still."

"They're just letting you and Alby hear everything?" I asked.

"Kid," she said, placing her hand on my arm. "They're not expecting us to live through this. They plan to kill us and pin the hijacking on us. Already they've got a bomb threat on a note in your handwriting, and your voice on a phone call making demands to the NTSB."

Not to mention the letter I'd written to Judge Cheevers with the false threat to bomb a plane in the hopes that my newly erratic behavior would convince him to revisit the custody arrangement. *Crap.* "And what about him?" I pointed to Cinderblock.

"They think I'm on their side," he answered for Flo. "They thought I'd been busted and was being extradited back to L.A. That's why I was pretending to be an escorted prisoner. And that's why, I might add, no one has been pounding on the door of the cockpit."

Just then, someone pounded on the door of the cockpit. We all jumped, startled. Officer Ned hit his head on the knobs of the cockpit ceiling and winced. Malcolm retreated all the way back into the cargo bay at the base of the access ladder. Flo looked through the peephole and opened the door.

Alby Madison stepped inside and closed the door behind her. "Your turn," she told Flo. Flo bundled her hair atop her head as best she could to try and make herself presentable, then moved to walk out the door.

"Wait!" I whispered. "Where are you going?"

"They're having us take turns tending to the cabins. They want the passengers to get a good look at us in order to bolster their story later on, is my guess. Not that it matters; half of them are panting for breath due to hypoxia."

"Wait, that was a fake decompression just to get the plane to dive. There was never any real loss of oxygen," I said.

"I know—and good one, by the way—but try telling them that."

"And they want one of us locked in the cockpit at all times, too, so it will appear to the fighter pilots that we have control of the aircraft," Alby explained. "They can't hear us because all communication has been shut down for some reason." I tried to look innocent.

"Here I go," Flo said.

"Wait," Officer Ned said. "Don't forget the nitro tabs. What good are they gonna do?"

"They can't hurt," she shrugged. "I've already spiked their coffee pot with half my stash; OxyContin, Xanax, beta-blockers, and that migraine medication. So far all it's done is make them fight with each other. Now, these nitro tabs oughta push them into some serious symptoms."

"You're gonna give them heart attacks," Officer Ned warned.

"Here's to hoping," Flo said, and started for the door. I put my arm out to stop her, my eyes pleading. "I'll be fine, kid," she promised me. She sounded so certain it made my heart hurt.

CHAPTER 17

Once Flo left we were all silent for a moment, digesting the information. Alby broke the silence. "Flo tells me you're Roy Coleman's granddaughter," she said. I nodded wanly. Everyone at WorldAir had known my grandfather Roy, even the CEO of the company. "A friend of mine interns for the law office that he used to file all his patents," she added.

That's right, I remembered. Alby is a third-year law student. I perked up with a sad smile. Malcolm emerged halfway through the hatch again, and I absently stroked Beefheart's sweet head.

"Uh, I'm sorry to hear he'd passed. He had quite a portfolio. What did you do with the shares that he left you?" she asked, trying to allay the quiet in the confined area.

I was deep in thought. How were we going to get out of this? Don't freak out, *figure* it out. Malcolm was up for conversation, though. "What shares?" he asked Alby.

"Her grandfather left her his shares of the company."

"What company?"

"WorldAir, of course. What company did you think I meant?"

Malcolm nudged my calf and said, "April, I think you want to pay attention to this."

"What?"

"This lady says your grandfather left you some shares in this company."

"What?" I directed my attention to Alby.

Alby eyed me quizzically. "Didn't you know?"

"What?" Evidently I was having trouble coming up with different words.

"April, your grandfather created a lot of useful inventions. He even holds the patent on the fuse that was the legacy of that plane wreck in Sioux City . . . ."

"1989!" Malcolm said. "Sioux City, Iowa, DC-10, a faulty engine fan disk disintegrated and blew shrapnel that severed all three hydraulic lines by the tail-mounted engine and disabled the aircraft's entire hydraulic system."

"The pilots lost all flight control," I remembered. "They had to attempt to minimize the crash landing by using engine thrust only. It was almost impossible to do. It's a miracle anyone at all survived, let alone over half the people on board." To this day, the pilot of that plane, Alfred C. Haynes, is one of the few who inspires my faith in the profession.

"Yes, honey," Alby spoke in a deliberate tone. "Your grandfather invented the fuse that prevents any catastrophic loss of hydraulic fluid, so a crash like that can never happen again. Didn't you know that?"

"No," I answered, bewildered.

"Your mother never told you? The papers must have been sent to . . . ." Then she clapped her hand over her mouth. "Your mother!"

"They were sent to my mother?" I asked.

"No! I just remembered. Your mother doesn't have custody of you! She's not your primary physical custodian. The papers were probably sent to . . . ."

Ash Manning! That bastard!

Officer Ned had to hold me back from busting through the door to try and bust open Ash's head. "Calm down, April, listen to what else she has to say."

"There's nothing else I can say," Alby said. "I don't have access to her grandfather's file. Not even April has access to his file. The only person who does is her legal custodian . . . oh, and her guardian ad litem."

Kathy Landry! I fumed. I turned to charge out the door once again. Officer Ned and Alby moved to stop me, but that proved unnecessary because I was already halted by a glimpse of something in my periphery—the unmistakable designer pattern of a Louis Vitton bag. It was wedged under the jumpseat reserved for deadheading pilots. Ash Manning was deadheading this flight. Ash Manning always carried the bags for that hollow-boned dung beetle he called a girlfriend!

I grabbed the strap of the bag and gave it a mighty tug, marveling at how strong it held. The bag remained pinched between the jumpseat and the fuselage. Alby reached over and grasped the second strap, and with a heave we were able to pull it free.

"What are you doing?" asked Officer Ned.

"This is Kathy's giant carpetbagger purse." I unsnapped the clasp, unzipped all the compartments, and yanked it open. Seriously, it was half the size of a golf bag. As a designer purse it must have cost more than a small car. In the side compartments were several legal files, which, upon cursory glance, proved to be her pending guardian ad litem cases. As a corporate attorney for WorldAir, Kathy's standing as a guardian ad litem registered with the Fulton County family court system not only helped fulfill her firm's quota of pro bono work, it evidently also raked in a nice side income for her, judging by the exorbitant tacked-on fees she extorted from the terrified parents of her charges. Believe me, a GAL's power holds heavy sway with judges, it was rare when someone challenged their recommendation. Malcolm's father's successful discrediting of Kathy's recommendation was a rare and wonderful thing. I flipped through the files and caught sight of a few heartbreaking faxes from parents who were tearfully flummoxed by Kathy's stupefying recommendations. ("Their mother is married to a registered sex offender, how can you give her custody of my sons?" "Little Nadine's father is on parole for manslaughter, please tell me your custody recommendation is a mistake!") As heartlessly as Kathy brandished her power, she was equally anal in her recordkeeping, and the files included copies of the checks and money transfers for the bribes she'd received to garner her favor. I found my own sizeable file and flipped it open—no canceled checks or copies of money transfers, instead there was an inch-thick folder of strange legal documents bearing my grandfather's name.

I handed the folder to Alby. "Can you look at this and tell me what it means?"

She quickly scanned the contents of the folder. "April, your grandfather licensed WorldAir with the use of his patent, and he directed all the funds from the royalties into a trust on your behalf. You were supposed to begin receiving graduated payments every month starting on your fifteenth birthday."

"Payments? What payments? How much are the payments?"

"A hundred and seventy-five thousand dollars."

"A hundred and seventy-five thousand dollars?"

"A month."

"A month?"

Malcolm whistled through his teeth. Officer Ned clutched his chest like the news had punched him there. Cinderblock kept quiet, his eyes behind his bottle glasses, faultily focused on the horizon. For my part, I was thinking of those nights I spent sleeping on patio cushions on the floor of Ash's laundry room, and the days I spent foraging for food through crew rooms and flight lounges, and that instant, right then, when I was wearing discarded old uniform pieces patched together from the lost and found. All of this when I had money?

"Why wasn't my mother included in this trust?"

"That's a good question. Originally it was set up for your dad, and when he died—" she reached out to touch my arm in sympathy "—it should have been passed to his surviving spouse. I don't know why it skipped her and went straight to you."

"They weren't married," I said.

"Say again?"

"My parents never married."

"Ah, well, that explains that."

I crouched down to stroke Beefheart's head again. Today was my fifteenth birthday and I'd had two people try to kill me so far today alone, not to mention the attempt weeks ago. I looked up at Cinderblock, who was trying to seem engrossed in the horizon. "Hey, you . . . uh, Hugh. Hugh!" I called. "What's going on? I know you know."

Officer Ned looked at his former partner expectantly.

"I'm really not at liberty to . . . ." Cinderblock began.

"Hugh, if you don't start talking I'll throw you off this plane myself! Don't think I don't know how," Officer Ned warned.

"Okay," Cinderblock blustered. "The money is coming from the airline, both dirty and laundered. From WorldAir. As far as we've been able to tell. Regarding the minor," he hooked his thumb to indicate me, "all I know is what I've overheard, and that is something about something set to expire, and they need to get her out of the way or else something reverts to something, blah blah blah. I don't know."

I was starting to get insulted that he hadn't paid closer attention, considering they were plotting someone's murder—my murder! What are these undercover operations like, anyway, do they just let the criminals go nuts, kill anyone they want, and scoop

up the poop afterward to mash a case together? Take the imposter Brighton McPherson, whose hitman activities seemed to be
gamely tolerated in exchange for being an informant. I was starting to see why Officer Ned may have been overlooked for a job
like this one. This would never sit well with him.

"I think I know what's happening," Alby said. "The license on
the patent expired three years ago, April, but WorldAir is still acting as though they have rights to it. This money being laundered
all this time . . . I think I know whose money it is."

"Whose?" Malcolm, Officer Ned, and I all asked in unison.

"April," she said gently, taking me by the shoulders and looking
me in the eye, "I think the money . . . is yours."

"What? *My* money? I don't have any money!"

"Well, yeah," Malcolm piped in, "now that Ash and Kathy are
stealing it all."

And then it all made sense. The ridiculous custody battle, the
vicious, lying, succubus of a sociopathic guardian ad litem, the
zeal with which Ash pursued the title of primary physical custodian (and of course his simultaneous complete and utter lack of
concern about my welfare). All of that ensured he'd become the
legal executor of my estate, an estate that no one seemed to know
I had except Ash and Kathy.

"Why would a money-laundering ring go to all this trouble
just for a hundred and seventy-five thousand a month?" I asked. I
mean, it was a lot of money to me, but it didn't seem worth creating a crime family over, or murdering people over, or bombing
airplanes over for that matter.

"April, I don't think you understand," Alby explained, her
voice patient. "We are not just talking about your monthly trust
payments. We are also talking about the control of the patent,
licensing fees, and your grandfather's shares in the company.
Together all this probably creates a sizeable chunk of ownership
in the company."

"What company?" I asked. This was too unreal seeming.

"*WorldAir!*" Malcolm, Officer Ned, and Alby all said at once.

A stunned silence descended on the cockpit—or, actually there could have been noise in there, but I was just too stunned to hear it. Then Flo knocked on the cockpit door to signal it was Alby's turn to take over wet-nurse duties in the cabin. When the door was closed, Flo informed us that half the band of hijackers had become convinced they were having a stroke and had accessed the emergency medical kit in the passenger cabin to down even more nitro tabs and take turns hooking themselves up to the defibrillator. The other half, which included Kathy and Ash, had become so paranoid of the others' intentions that they'd actually come to physical blows and had to be separated by some well-meaning passengers.

By now all of the hijackers were certain each was being double-crossed by the other, and the last Flo saw they were all eyeing each other with hissing suspicion from different corners of the cabin. Any remaining non-criminal flight attendants stayed petrified in their seats at the spectacle, and the pilots had passed out from constricted blood flow due to the fact that they'd been hogtied for the last half hour.

The passengers themselves were still mostly utterly ignorant of what was transpiring, other than the fact that this was a very odd and eventful flight, seeing as how guns kept going off (or maybe it was firecrackers, or minor explosions in the engine) and dead air marshals were being stuffed in the coat closet (or maybe it's just another drunk guy) and oxygen masks were being dropped and giant life rafts were being deployed (okay, that actually happened) (right?). Any communication between Ramona and the lower galley was done through the intercom system, not the PA system, so it was beyond the earshot of passengers, and anyone who had gotten themselves shot and/or killed had done so in a galley or cross-aisle outside the direct view of passengers. I'm not saying every single passenger was completely oblivious to the nefarious goings-on of WorldAir flight 1021, but those who weren't knew to stay out of the way, and those who were just kept ringing their call buttons, wondering why the snack cart was taking so long. Anyone left over was experiencing the placebo effect of fake hypoxia and were therefore harmless for the time being.

"Have at it," Flo told Alby. "It ain't pretty." She gratefully lit another cigarette and dragged deeply before noticing my expression. "What?" she asked. I didn't answer.

"Cinderblock . . . I mean, Hugh," I said, passing him the coordinates that had been faxed earlier. "Can you read these and get us down?"

He squinted at the paper and finally answered. "Yes and no," he said.

"What do you mean, 'yes and no'?" I asked.

"Yes, I can read these coordinates, and no, I can't get us down," he said.

"Why? All you have to do is punch in the numbers," I said.

"I'm aware of that, young lady. I'm also aware that these coordinates—" he threw them at the floorboard on the copilot's side "—are wrong."

PART XI

THE LANDING

We tried to revive the pilots, but to no avail. They had been untied by a helpful passenger who'd discovered them on the way to the lavatory, and the pilots then each made themselves a cup of coffee from the pot of Flo's pharmacological cocktail. It wasn't a matter of shaking them awake. They were awake, if staring straight ahead, gritting your teeth, shaking like a hummingbird, and sweating like a silverback gorilla could be considered "awake." The issue was that their condition was useless. ("Tell me something new," Flo snorted sardonically.)

The hijackers had long been reduced to minimal threats. Flo's gun was empty and the other gun, the one taken from the air marshal, had been flushed down the lavatory toilet by Ash, who had become convinced Kathy meant to kill him with it. I'm sure he wasn't far off the mark with that. Because, as the spouse of my official custodial parent, Kathy stood to inherit my grandfather's trust the minute Ash was out of the way. The only glitch was that I had to be out of the way first in order for Ash to inherit it himself. I don't know if he understood that this was part of her plan or not, but I was certain his greedy little hooks were all over the scheme to steal my grandfather's patent money and launder it through the Caymans. That was a no-brainer.

I sent Flo and Alby through the cabin to see if they could find a pilot traveling nonrevenue, or any facsimile thereof who could help us make an instrument landing of the plane. No such luck. *Seriously?* I thought. It's like you're buried in this element when you're trying to duck the radar, but when you need it, *poof!*, gone except for the hallucinating contingent strapped to their seats in the forward galley.

Flo had gotten hold of the imposter Brighton McPherson's cell phone and was yelling "Representative!" into the mouthpiece. She hung up in exasperation.

Agent Kowalski:

Why didn't you dial me back?

April Manning:

Because your number is blocked, Agent Kowalski. Believe me, I tried.

Investigator DeAngelo:

So what did you do?

April Manning:

I dialed 411 and asked for the number of the Circle K at the corner of Manhattan Beach Boulevard and Inglewood Avenue.

Investigator DeAngelo:

Uh . . . say again?

April Manning:

I called the Circle K at the corner of Manhattan Beach Boulevard and Inglewood Avenue. Thankfully, LaVonda Morgenstern answered the phone.

"Hi, LaVonda!" I said. "It's April, remember from a few weeks ago? When you called 911 for me?"

"Well, hi there, honey pie!" she shrieked into the phone. "How are you doin'? You know I went by the hospital to see how you were holding up after I finished talkin' to the police. They said you were a runaway, but I told them, ain't no runaway situation here, this be an *abuse* situation here—"

"LaVonda, seriously, it's so good to hear your voice—" It really was. "—but I need you to do me a favor, please. Do you think you can?"

"What is it, darlin'?" Her voice took on a tone of seriousness. "Wait, let me lock the door, some fool be tryin' to come in here and buy something. I swear, some *people. Get out!*" she yelled at the intruding customer. "Can't you see we in *distress*? Okay, child, just tell me what you need."

I asked her to please open her laptop ("It already open, girl") and pull up Google maps to see what the nearest airport was, about twelve hundred miles west of Atlanta, Georgia. "Okay, got it," she said. "Albuquerque Sunport International Airport. Now what?"

"Can you Google the coordinates for landing an L-1011 at that airport?"

As before, she did as I asked without question. "How do you spell 'coordinates'?"

I told her the wrong spelling, but Google suggested the correction and she was able to bring up the search results. "Okay, there is a jumble of letters and numbers here," she began, "I'm just gonna call them out to you, okay? N three five degrees—I think that's 'degrees,' right? The cute little circle at the top? I know if we were talking about weather that would mean 'degrees.'"

"It does," I clarified.

"Right." Then LaVonda continued, " . . . two point four one; W one oh six degrees three six point five five . . . ." I recited the numbers aloud to Cinderblock as LaVonda recited them to me.

"T-O-R-A ten thousand, T-O-D-A ten thousand, A-S-D-A ten thousand," LaVonda continued, then said, "Wow, what is that sound? What is happenin' on your end of the phone, child?"

"Uh, LaVonda, I'm going to hand you over to my guy Hugh here," I told her, and Cinderblock took the phone and gave her a gruff greeting. Officer Ned positioned himself in the copilot's seat. I could still hear LaVonda's loud voice asking about that noise on my end of the phone. But I didn't have time to answer. I had to get back down to the lower galley, because that noise was the sound of a bomb that had just exploded.

CHAPTER 18

"Malcolm!" I screamed as I crawled back through the avionics area and down the catwalk, because I realized with a choking panic that Malcolm was not at the foot of the access ladder anymore. "Malcolm!" I felt the plane make an autopilot dive in order to accommodate an altitude that could compensate for the decompression, a *real* decompression this time.

I saw that the hole in the bulkhead had been cleared of the camouflage and I stepped through, expecting to see a bombed-out war zone. But no, the galley appeared intact. I hopped into the lift and flipped the toggles to take me to the cabin above. When I opened the door, that's when I saw the war zone.

Passengers screamed as debris flew through the aisles toward the back of the plane. Oxygen masks flapped around in the wind like kelp on an active ocean bed. Passengers cried, screamed, lapsed into catatonic states, or flung their hands aloft like this was a roller coaster ride. By the time I stepped out of the lift, the plane had already completed its dive, once again to under fourteen thousand feet and the air was safe to breathe without an oxygen mask. When I exited the galley, I saw that all the passengers from the D zone had been relocated to the forward cabins, and where the aft left door should have been, a sizeable hole gaped instead.

"Malcolm!" I screamed again, my voice cracking with terror. "Malcolm!"

I felt a hand on my arm. I turned to see that it was Malcolm, wearing an oxygen mask. Captain Beefheart was wearing one as well, still strapped to his chest. And Malcolm was not so much touching my arm as he was grabbing it.

"Sit down!" he yelled over the rush of the air and the engines.

I did as he said and buckled myself into a seat. Malcolm strapped an oxygen mask over my mouth and nose and motioned for me to breathe in and out slowly. I wondered why he thought he needed to instruct me on how to breathe, and the thought made me giggle uncontrollably. I reached out to slap him playfully and he caught my hands, folded them into my lap, and held them there. I continued to giggle until suddenly things didn't seem too funny anymore. The aircraft leveled out and it was safe to take off the oxygen masks, though few of the passengers did.

I took a few deep breaths and pulled off my mask. *Wow*, I thought, *so that's what hypoxia feels like.*

Malcolm pulled off his mask and I saw that Alby sat in the seat next to him. We were the only three passengers in D zone, plus Captain Beefheart. You have to count Captain Beefheart.

"What happened?" I cried.

The digital screen on the bomb had started to count down again, Malcolm explained. There was no time to clamber back through avionics to tell me about it, so he and Alby worked to secure the bomb in the position that, according to the flight attendant manual, would create the least damage in such a situation. In this case, it was against the left aft door of the cabin. So Malcolm and Alby gingerly placed the device there and enlisted the passengers to help by handing over their carry-on bags, blankets, neck pillows, and anything else that could be stacked against the device to create a buffer against the cabin and direct the explosion outward. They finished by using seatbelt extensions, neckties, earphone wires, and anything else they could use to fashion a webbing to direct the blast outward against the door instead of inward against the fuselage. After that it was just a matter of waiting . . . then *boom!*

Alby and Malcolm had been so masterful at situating the bomb that all it destroyed, literally, was the aft left door, which flew off the body of the plane and fell to the ground like a big metal flower petal twisting in the wind. Now that the altitude had been stabilized, the result was a lot like what it had been when we were in the lower galley and had the door open—loud and blustery, only minus the dog and friends jumping out of the plane.

I unclicked my seatbelt and stood. "Where are you going?" Malcolm asked.

"Back to the cockpit," I said. He told me to wait for him. Alby indicated that she would stay in D zone to ensure that no passengers stepped off the plane and into the abyss while looking for the lavatory or anything. At that, Malcolm and I made our way to the mid galley through the outstretched arms of the minority of passengers still clueless enough to hope for a packet of peanuts or something.

We took the lift down and then ascended to the cockpit through the hatch in the floor of the flight deck in order to avoid the drug-overdosing cluster of (now-ineffectual) hijackers congregated in first class.

"What was that?" Cinderblock asked.

"The bomb," Malcolm said, sounding amazingly calm.

"I figured," he responded, equally calm. It occurred to me that this was now our way of handling things. This had to be normal for now, because if we stopped for a second to reflect on the severity of the situation, we would be as useless as the gaggle of hissing idiots directly on the other side of the cockpit door.

"April, child, you okay?" I heard LaVonda's voice project from the speaker of the imposter Brighton McPherson's cell phone. "Talk to me, child!"

"LaVonda!" I hollered. "I'm good. Thanks. Thanks so much. So good to hear you."

"Likewise, lovely!"

Cinderblock had entered the coordinates as LaVonda repeated them to him from the Google search results. Now all we had to do was hope that, for once, the Internet wasn't a big bog of lies and misguidance in this particular instance.

"What do you think?" I asked Officer Ned.

"What I think," he answered, "is that you ought to take over this copilot's seat." He began the painful process of raising his six-foot-five frame from the cramped pilot seat.

"I don't know how to fly a jet!" I protested.

"April, next to Hugh here—and I say this with more skepticism of his abilities than yours—you know more than anyone what to do. Now, I'm gonna take the jumpseat behind you. Malcolm, you strap yourself into the navigator's seat and hold on. Flo, go out and make sure those fools out there are buckled in, then take the jumpseat at the forward door. This is probably gonna be a hard landing."

That turned out to be a euphemism, and as you know, I hate euphemisms.

CHAPTER 19

Cinderblock did the best he could, but he was operating on the knowledge of an expired small-craft pilot's license and the eyesight of a vampire bat. That said, at least the tower of the Albuquerque Sunport International Airport completely suspended traffic when they saw us coming on the radar and couldn't get a response from the cockpit. When the L-1011 slammed into the runway, it was probably testimony to Cinderblock's abilities that the only thing that broke off was the tail section of the aircraft, which somersaulted like a terrible metal tumbleweed and came to rest against an abandoned Eastern Airlines hangar. Luckily, Malcolm and Alby had relocated all the passengers from the tail zone of the aircraft to the front of the plane, far away from the missing aft door, leaving as big a margin of empty rows as possible.

So, as you know, there were no casualties from the tail zone. You're welcome.

When the rest of the fuselage finally came to a rest in a weed field parallel to the runway, the flight attendants barely had time to deploy the escape slides before the wings ignited and the aircraft burst into flames. I opened the cockpit door to see Flo holding the assist handle and directing people to "Jump and slide!" down the chute to safety. I was relieved to see Malcolm, with little Captain Beefheart still tucked into his improvised baby sling, at the bottom of the chute, helping people from the slide and directing them to run away from the plane. And I saw Ash, of course, just running away. I reached behind Flo, unhooked her hand from the assist handle, and hurled her down the slide. (It's all in the leverage.) *If these people can't find their own way out*, I thought, *they don't deserve to have Flo die trying to help them.*

I could hear the other, non-hijacker flight attendants dutifully calling out the crash commands to the passengers in order to direct their safe evacuation. ("Leave everything!") Many of the passengers had already wisely crouched down to armrest level to feel their way out of the plane. I coughed and covered my mouth with my sleeve. Ash had already left, of course.

Kathy, though, lay a few rows from me, slumped over her tray table, weakly mewling for help. I thought about it, the one wrong step—in instead of out, this way instead of that. Should I take it? I can't really explain what happened next, except to say I suddenly found myself at her side, unbuckling her seatbelt and yanking her up. Just then another explosion racked the cabin, and I felt a blast of scalding air hit my face.

Did I tell you that Officer Ned could move like lightning? I'm sure I did. Because faster than the flames could reach me, Officer Ned had his good arm around me and was running down the aisle, half lifting, half dragging me to the forward door. He dove us both out the opening, only to find that the slide had deflated. So he grabbed at the flapping sheet of rubber as we fell, trying to create friction to slow us down, then turned to ensure that his body fully broke my fall.

A fleet of emergency vehicles had already been dispatched, and EMTs descended on me and Officer Ned mere moments after we hit the ground. The strong arms of the medical personnel pulled me to safety as others carried Officer Ned in the opposite direction. I called after him, but he didn't answer me. I saw them put him in an ambulance. He was as limp as the slide hanging from the aircraft. Before they sped off, Old Cinderblock jumped into the ambulance at Officer Ned's side and closed the door behind him.

When the EMTs had me a safe distance from the burning aircraft, they determined that I wasn't really all that hurt but for some sore lungs and all the hair framing my face scorched away. As they adjusted the oxygen mask over my face, I swore I heard someone calling my name from the weeds in the field nearby. I followed the sound, against the urgent advice of the EMTs, and rifled through the brush until the sound grew stronger.

"April! Honey child!" LaVonda's voice called. "What was that sound? Answer me, girl!"

I picked up the imposter Brighton McPherson's cell phone and brought it to my ear. "Hi, LaVonda!" I cried.

"Oh, I am so happy to hear your voice," she gasped with relief. "Lord, girl, what was that?"

"That? That was just the plane crashing," I told her. Then, for like the fiftieth time today, I'm embarrassed to say, I burst into sobs.

LaVonda continued to patter to me comfortingly as the EMTs lifted me once again to transport me to safety. It was then that I noticed something looped around my elbow as I held the phone to my ear. *What's that?* I thought. *Lord, that's heavy.* I thought it was maybe a seat cushion tangled with my arm by the seatbelt, it was that big and heavy. But when I entered the ambulance and took a seat next to a number of other passengers with minimal injuries, I noticed that it was not a seat cushion at all. It was Kathy's purse. Her main purse. The one big enough to carry a bunch of severed heads.

CHAPTER 20

Preliminary Accident Report, cont.
WorldAir flight 1021, April 1, 2013
Present at transcript:
April May Manning, unaccompanied minor
Detective Jolette Henry, Albuquerque Police Department
Investigator Peter DeAngelo, NTSB
Investigator Anthony Kowalski, FBI
and
Alan Bertram, CEO, WorldAir

Investigator DeAngelo:
Well, Agent Kowalski, what do you think of this?
Agent Kowalski:
I don't know what to think of this.
Alan Bertram, CEO, WorldAir:
Gentleman, sorry to barge in, but I wanted to give you the list of fatalities from this disaster today. I'm going to need to make a statement to the press as soon as possible, and I wanted to know if you'd concluded anything from your interviews of the survivors.

Agent Kowalski:
The death count is only five? That's impressive.
Investigator DeAngelo:
Officer Ned Rockwell, Florence Davenport, Alby Madison, Hugh Newman, and April Manning.
April Manning:
I think you're jumping the gun there.
Alan Bertram:
Oh, right. Four casualties. Let me correct that . . . . So, what have you concluded so far in regard to what caused the accident?
Investigator DeAngelo:
I'll tell you what I've concluded. I have concluded that this girl is diabolical. She's a juvenile criminal who hijacked and bombed an aircraft and now she actually thinks she can con her way out of it with this crazy story.
April Manning:
Malcolm Colgate will back me up.
Investigator DeAngelo:
Right, another unaccompanied minor. Who cares what he has to say.
Agent Kowalski:
Hey, hold on . . . we haven't even tried to corroborate anything.
Investigator DeAngelo:
I don't have to hold on. I have the authority to conclude this investigation based on my findings. If you don't agree with me, Agent Kowalski, then you can submit your own findings to your own bureau.

[sound of cell phone ringing.]

Mr. Bertram:
Please excuse me, gentlemen. I need to step down the hall and take this call.

Investigator DeAngelo:
Keep your hands on the table, April.
April Manning:
It's just a cell phone. I'll put it on speaker.
Mr. Alan Bertram (via speakerphone):
Kathy, sweetheart, darling, don't be upset. I had no idea the bomb was on your plane. Do you think I'd let you make the money run if I'd known the bomb was on your plane? Huh, honey? Pumpkin? Hello? Kathy? Helloooo.
Mr. Alan Bertram:
I'm back, gentleman. Sorry about that. So, am I safe to make a statement that the preliminary investigation finds this girl responsible?
Agent Kowalski:
April, whose phone is that in your hand?
April Manning:
It belongs to Kathy Landry. I have her purse right here.
Agent Kowalski:
Detective Henry, please cuff Mr. Bertram and escort him outside. Don't forget to read him his rights.
Detective Henry:
Mr. Bertram, please turn around and put your hands behind your back.
Mr. Bertram:
What's the meaning of this? This is preposterous! Stop this immediately! Investigator DeAngelo, do something!
Investigator DeAngelo:
Uh . . . what do you think you're doing, Agent Kowalski?
Agent Kowalski:
I'm arresting the CEO of WorldAir. I have him on tape talking to a known felon referencing a money run and the bombing of an aircraft.
Investigator DeAngelo:

What tape?

Agent Kowalski:

The tape of this *transcript*, you dimwad.

Investigator DeAngelo:

Well, uh, we don't have any conclusive evidence that . . . .

Agent Kowalski:

How's this for conclusive evidence: I've been running an undercover operation for the past three years. My main agent, whose identity I don't care to disclose right now—

April Manning:

It's Old Cinderblock, just say it. His cover is kinda blown.

Agent Kowalski:

Fine, my agent, Hugh Newman, was kind enough to fill me in on some things before I arrived here today.

Investigator DeAngelo:

Hugh Newman is on the fatality list!

Agent Kowalski:

Are you really that thick? Newman *made* this list. Nobody died on that plane today. We just needed to see how you'd act when you thought all the witnesses were out of the way.

Investigator DeAngelo:

What do you mean, how I'd act? What have I got to do with any of this?

Agent Kowalski:

Investigator DeAngelo, turn around and put your hands behind your back. You have the right to remain silent . . . .

PART XII

THE TERM PAPER

The Five People I Admire Most
by
April Mae Manning

First, I appreciate how this term paper is asking me to make a list. I love lists. Second, I apologize for taking so long to finish this assignment. It took me a while to realize I had five people in my life who deserve my admiration. But in light of recent events, I've come to see that very differently. Today I now believe there are more than five people, even, which may inspire me to make a few lists within a list (which is awesome):

1. **Roy Coleman**

I admire my granddaddy Roy Coleman because he was a modest man who loved to labor with his hands. This is where he differed from his old friend and WorldAir CEO Alan Bertram. They both started out as engineers, both hired on the same day at WorldAir, but where Roy Coleman liked to push up his shirtsleeves and put in an honest day's work, Mr. Bertram liked to climb the corporate ladder by stealing inventions from his oldest friend to skip as many rungs as possible on the way to the top.

Some of my favorite memories are from the Sundays I used to spend with my granddaddy Roy while I helped him tinker with engines and test his inventions in the large barn in the back of his property. "To work is to pray," he used to say to me.

My granddaddy died when the jack supporting the vintage Ford Rambler he was restoring collapsed and crushed his chest. But before that, he had quietly amassed a portfolio containing escalating chunks of company stock bought with the fees from a number of patents on a number of inventions that had been licensed by WorldAir. Before Granddaddy Roy died, he had never once even asked to see this portfolio, and afterward his old (backstabbing) friend Mr. Bertram had been entrusted to pay the renewal and licensing fees into a trust that had long ago been set up for my father and me. Evidently Mr. Bertram thought that since Roy Coleman was dead it would be better to pocket that money instead, but not before laundering it along with the other funds he was stealing from WorldAir. He didn't think anyone would notice. He was wrong about that.

2. **Officer Ned Rockwell**

It turns out Officer Ned used to be a linebacker for a professional football team, the name of which I won't mention because he's asked me not to. Anyway, this explains why he had the ability to move with the speed of a cheetah when circumstances called for it, what with his innate athletic reflexes and all. His football career lasted exactly one season before he was fired for beating the crap out of two teammates after he'd discovered they were running a dog-fighting ring. Officer Ned asked me not to mention that part, too. He said it wasn't important, but we saw that differently.

By my count, Officer Ned saved my life several times, once when he threw himself in front of the bullets heading for my face, and again when he pulled me out of the burning fuselage of the crashed WorldAir flight 1021. And probably again when he broke my fall once we dove out the door together, only to be confronted by a deflated escape slide. He also saved the life of my friend Malcolm Colgate, not to mention Malcolm's emotional support dog, Captain Beefheart. Malcolm and Beefheart are two of the most precious things I hold dear. If I'd lost them, I don't know if I'd have been able to go on, so I count this as an official fourth time Officer Ned saved me. He seems uncomfortable with my gratitude, though.

Following the crash, he was in a coma for a day and a half. When he awoke, the three first things he said were:

- "Are April and Malcolm okay?"
- "Where are my boots?"
- "Flo, put out that damn cigarette, *this is a hospital*!"

He'll deny it, but Flo swears this was the correct order of his post-coma statements, and she should know because she was there for a day and a half sleeping in an upholstered armchair next to his bedside, claiming to be his "patient advocate," and demanding he receive the quality pain medication and not that "generic crap."

Considering his injuries, I'm impressed that Officer Ned only spent a week in the hospital recovering from them. But he kept reminding me this was not the first time he'd been shot, and haranguing that the worst of his hurt was due to the fall from the aircraft. It caused his other lung to collapse (the first lung had collapsed when he'd been shot in the ribs). "It didn't help that you landed right on top of me," he said. I didn't remind him that he'd made sure to break my fall. Now that I'm a major shareholder in WorldAir, I plan to recommend him to replace the head of company security. I hope he doesn't turn it down like he did with the promotion he was finally offered from the Atlanta Police Department. First, he can't be worse at the job than the present WorldAir head of security is (I mean, all this happened right under his nose), and second, I plan to recommend LaVonda Morgenstern as his second in command (I can't *wait* to see the combustion created by the chemistry of those two). How awesome would it be for me to be *Officer Ned's boss*? I seriously can't wait for that day. I might even give back his badge I stole.

Anyway, even shot up and hopped full of painkillers, Officer Ned's first thought is to help others before himself. I think it's another reflex with him. A rare and amazing reflex worthy of my admiration.

The boots, by the way, had belonged to his father, who was a motorcycle cop.

3. **Malcolm Colgate**
Some would say Malcolm is my only friend, but they would be wrong. More specifically, he is my only friend my age. I admire him because he's brilliant for the following reasons (a list within a list!):

- He was the one who noticed that Flo had overheard the hijackers talking about how the NTSB had my voice making demands on tape in a telephone call. "How would the *hijackers* know that?" he asked. And he was right, of course; how would the hijackers know about that phone call— unless someone at the National Transportation Safety Board told them.
- He is the one who suggested I filibuster during my statement to the authorities to see if I could flush out who the traitor was. We knew it had to be somebody from the FBI or the NTSB, or even WorldAir. That's why my statement took ten million years to make. It was to give Old Cinderblock, otherwise known as undercover detective Hugh Newman, time to convince the authorities to send a bogus fatality list to the CEO of WorldAir. I even had to impersonate the symptoms of mild shock, not that they cared. In the end it was bigger than even we thought, and our brains can go pretty far out there.
- He is almost as knowledgeable as I am when it comes to aviation disasters.
- He is also the one who persuaded his father to get his attorney to hound the police regarding the microchip implanted in Beefheart. (I swear, is it me? Or are the

police sometimes as deaf as dirt when it comes to anything an unaccompanied minor has to say?) It turned out there was a ring of prisoners in the Fulton County Pen—one of whom was a previous CEO of WorldAir serving four years for embezzlement—who were calibrating the microchips in the support dog–training program to convey the bank account numbers and other information needed to wash the funds in Grand Cayman. It turned out that those microchips are electromagnetic, so they can easily be used as a sensor, as well, and also easily (Mr. Alan Bertram thought) be used to kill a giant bird with one stone. I seriously look forward to the day Malcolm gets to testify against him during the criminal trial against the CEO of WorldAir for attempting to bomb one of his own aircraft.

- He also got his father's attorney to file an official contempt charge against Kathy Landry for gross misconduct as a guardian ad litem. It's a tiny drop in the bucket of the other charges pending against her right now, but it's supremely satisfying for me and Malcolm—not to mention Captain Beefheart. To think it was her idea to enlist unwitting children of divorce—whose welfare she'd been entrusted with by the court!—and their innocent emotional support animals in this criminal scheme. "What a bottom fish," as Flo would say.

4. Florence "Flo" Beulah Butterfield Schnieder Chang Davenport

I admire Flo because she's sixty-seven years old, has seen it all and is surprised by none of it, not even a nonrev runaway who lives in the sky. She is the kind of person who can kill a man, come across a bomb, get shot in the head (pretty much), outsmart hijackers (one of whom was her estranged son), and just continue on like it was any other day. Oh, and let's not forget the plane wreck. She stepped out of the escape slide like it was a limo door. For her the only personal casualty from the day was the big bun she styled her hair in. Today she has a cute haircut she calls "The Meg Ryan." We got separated after the ambulance ride back to the concourse of Albuquerque International Airport. I told her to please go check on Officer Ned, and she did as I asked, but not before going through Kathy Landry's purse to produce her cell phone and point out a few interesting names on the contact list. WorldAir CEO Alan Bertram's private cell number was listed under "Old Sucker."

"How do you know Alan Bertram's private cell phone number?"

"Kid, let's just say he and I go back. I've been around, you know" was all she'd admit.

She reminded me to filibuster my incident report as long as possible like Malcolm suggested I do in order to give Old Cinderblock some time to work some angles from his end. "And I don't have to tell you—do I, kid?—to keep in mind that there might be one or two sleepers left to deal with." She did not have to remind me.

This is why, when Investigator Peter DeAngelo of the NTSB stepped into the interrogation chamber, something clicked in my memory; it had to do with that slip of notepaper I'd pulled from Kathy's little purse after I escaped the car trunk. At the time, among the indecipherable scribbling and penciled notations, all I could make out were the words "angel" and "angels," but when I discovered the context the scribbling began to make more sense to me. First of all, one of the "angels" referred to Angels Among Us, the pet-rescue organization that unwittingly supplied the information mules for her money smuggling.

The other "angel" on the paper was not an angel at all, but "DeAngelo," as in Investigator Peter DeAngelo of the NTSB. I was able to get a good look at his badge when he first stepped into the interrogation chamber to speak with Detective Henry. Ah, I realized, Agent Kowalski had said he would relay my message to the NTSB, which also explains why the landing coordinates faxed to the cockpit were meant to nosedive us into the tarmac.

"Hello, April," he said when he finally turned to me. "I'm Investigator DeAngelo of the NTSB."

Hello, sleeper, I thought to myself as I shook his hand.

5. **Elizabeth Coleman Manning**

I admire my mother because, though she's not perfect, she did the absolute best she could given the circumstances, which were far from ideal. She married Ash in a misguided attempt to provide a father for me, and when that blew up in her face she fought with the ferocity of a grizzly bear to make things right. Not every (or hardly any) move she made in this regard helped matters, but considering the deck she had stacked against her, I'm in awe of the fact that she didn't snap like a turkey bone and just give up. Other mothers have cracked under a lot less, Alby told me. ("And she could be like mine," Malcolm said.) Also, I think it says something that, in the face of all this strife, she never once asked my granddaddy Roy to dip into my trust to help her out. I really do. It makes me remember the end of her sky stories, when she'd tell me right before I fell asleep, "Remember, April, I love you more than anything. I love you more than Grammy Mae, I love you more than Poppa Max, I love you more than Flo, I love you more than Ash. I love you more than I love myself, and I even love you more than you love *yourself.* I love you, I love you, I love you . . . " and those were the words I heard as I drifted off to sleep.

After seeing my three best friends almost make a no-parachute skydive from the lower galley of the L-1011 on my fifteenth birthday, I understand now how horrifying and helpless it feels when someone you love is in danger. My mother understood I faced a threat in her divorce situation, and she knew the threat was way greater than Ash Manning, but she didn't know what it was or why, for God's sake, I faced it. The most she could do was try to learn to navigate the bizarro world of family court, and that takes time, believe me. Alby has been studying family law for five years, and it won't be until next month when she finally takes the bar exam, "and even then you're just beginning to map the battleground," she says. That explains it pretty well, too. My mother was not even present at the right battleground. She was stuck in the real world, not the bizarro world of family law, where a mother's proclamations of love for her child are used as a weapon against her.

Case in point: Even though Ash was in prison awaiting trial for colluding with hijackers, the court still wouldn't return my custody to my mother. The reason? Despite everything, Kathy Landry was still my guardian ad litem and, get this, she had the gall to fire off a letter from her hospital bed recommending against returning me to my mother. Never mind that this shebeast had tried to kill me, *and* steal my trust fund by marrying my stepfather; never mind that my stepfather Ash Manning hasn't seen me since his idiot actions almost killed me and one hundred fifty other people, including himself; never mind that she was party to the bombing of an aircraft; never mind that she used her status as a court officer to further her money-smuggling agenda. Never mind any of this, because all of this was happing in *another* court. In the eyes of *family* court, Kathy still had a paper with Judge Cheevers's signature on it, and if there's anything judges hate, it's to have one of their bad decisions come back to slap them in the face. They hate it so much, in fact, that they'll invent reasons against having to admit the decision was ever bad in the first place.

In Judge Cheevers's case, all he did in response to my mother's petition for emergency custody was file a response that said, simply, "The court sees no reason to readdress custody."

It's a good thing I've gotten pretty talented at navigating battlegrounds myself. So I took Alby's advice and submitted a Petition for the Emancipation of a Minor on my own behalf. My mother is behind me on this. Some people would think this meant she was unfit to care for me, but we see that differently.

END.